ANOTHER CHANCE WITH LOVE

Blake Allwood

Another Chance With Love. Copyright © 2020 by Blake Allwood.
All Rights Reserved.

All rights reserved. No part of this book may be reproduced in any form or by any electronic or mechanical means including information storage and retrieval systems, without permission in writing from the author. The only exception is by a reviewer, who may quote short excerpts in a review.

Cover designed by Samrat Acharjee

This book is a work of fiction. Names, characters, places, and incidents either are products of the author's imagination or are used fictitiously. Any resemblance to actual persons, living or dead, events, or locales is entirely coincidental.

Blake Allwood
Visit my website at www.blakeallwood.com

Printed in the United States of America
Box Elder, SD

First Printing: July 2020

ISBN: 9798663165860
Library of Congress Control Number: 2021920415

Content Warnings:
Abuse
Child Abuse
Violence
Death or Dying
Kidnapping and Abduction
Murder

Titles by Blake Allwood:

<u>Transitions Series</u>
Aiden Inspired
Suzie Empowered
Bobby Transformed

<u>Chance Series</u>
Love By Chance (1)
Another Chance With Love (2)
Taking A Chance For Love (3)

<u>Big Bend Series</u>
Love's Legacy (1)
Love's Heirloom (2)
Love's Bequest (3)

<u>Romantic Series</u>
Romantic Renovations (1)
Romantic Rescue (2)
Romantic Recon (coming soon)

<u>Coming Home Series</u>
Tenacious

Purchase at:
readerlinks.com/mybooks/4515

Join Blake's email list to get advance notice of new books and receive his occasional newsletter:

blakeallwood.com

Thank you to the following people for their assistance:

Jo Bird - Editor
Kristopher Miller – Editor
Aryl Shanti - Editor
Julia Firlotte – Proof Reader
Renee Mizar – Proof Reader (2nd ed)

A special thank you goes to all my friends and family who supported me, I couldn't have done it without you.

And finally, an extra special thanks to my Husband who continues to tolerate me no matter how many of these rabbit holes I keep going down (and I seem to keep going down them).

A note from the author:

As I was finishing the final edit for this book, the Supreme Court of the United States ruled that it was no longer legal to fire someone just because they are LGBTQ+. I debated removing the parts of the story where Peter lost his job because his conservative boss saw him kissing his boyfriend.

Ultimately, I decided to leave it in, mostly because for all my life, and for the lives of many LGBTQ+ folks before me, losing a job because of your orientation was always a real possibility.

I dedicate this book to all LGBTQ people who have known this struggle. I also hope it stands as a reminder of all the years our community has had to fight for the basic rights that most people take for granted.

Trevor

"Lisa, how the hell am I supposed to raise a baby?" I asked with as much incredulity as I could muster.

"How the hell should I know?" she replied. "At least you have money. I have nothing. My parents even kicked me out when they heard I was pregnant."

That made my heart hurt. Lisa and I were friends long before we hooked up. "Damn, Lisa, have you spoken to them?"

"No, they cut me off completely, that's why I didn't come back to school this year."

The anger hit me like a ton of bricks. "You mean you were pregnant with *our* baby, your parents kicked you out, and you *still* wouldn't return my calls?"

Lisa stared down at her hands. "I was going to get an abortion, Trevor. I didn't want you to know."

"But you didn't!" I replied, still fuming that she'd chosen to go through all that on her own.

"I tried, but I couldn't go through with it," she continued, still staring at her hands. "I pulled up to the clinic and saw three people I went to church with protesting and I... I just couldn't."

I sighed, some of the anger leaking out of me. "You should've told me at least. I would've helped. Shit, at least I can help now."

The baby began to fuss in the carrier. Lisa reached down and patted his stomach as the tears rolled down her cheeks.

"When I couldn't go through with the abortion, I decided to give him up for adoption. But I chickened out when they told me you'd have to sign the paperwork. So, I was stuck, and I knew how I'd left you and..."

Her tears continued to flow.

I leaned back in my chair and ran my hands through my hair. This had all hit me out of the blue. Lisa and I had gotten drunk one night at the end of spring break, and being idiots, we'd ended up having sex. She left the next day, she stopped texting, stopped taking my calls, wouldn't return my emails... it sucked, and I missed her.

"We can do this together, you know," I said, even though my hands were still over my eyes.

Lisa was staring at the baby when I finally looked at her.

"No," she replied in a small voice. "I can't raise him. You're bisexual and... and... My parents would never forgive me for embarrassing them with a child out of wedlock. You know how religious they are."

I hmphed, ignoring the bisexual statement. I'd told her that before we'd gotten drunk and... well, and apparently made a baby. "They don't deserve you, Lisa." I spat out, then smiling said, "In some ways, they're worse than my parents."

A small but tentative smile crossed her lips as we began the same argument we'd been having since high school. Lisa's parents were strict Catholics, and mine were insane Baptists.

"What do you want me to do, Lisa?" I asked when she reached down and picked the infant up. This was the first time I'd seen him properly, and I lost track of the conversation immediately. He was so small, his little face scrunched up with an expression of discomfort. I could tell he was about to start wailing.

"My God, he's beautiful," I remarked, and Lisa looked at me in a strange way. "We made that?" I asked in shock.

"If I remember right, I did all the hard work," she said, and we were back to our snippy friendship like we hadn't been apart for nine-and-a-half months.

I chuckled. "I'd have helped if I'd known. Can I hold him?" I asked, feeling a strange stirring in my chest.

Lisa hesitated like she was afraid to let me, but then she handed him over. I'm lucky I didn't lose my shit right there. I nuzzled him, lost in all that this meant and all it would mean from this point on. He settled down in my arms, and I smiled. I could see some of my grandpa in his face. The second I spotted the resemblance, my own tears threatened to fall. My gregarious, left-wing nut of a grandpa would have loved this baby, and he'd have known exactly what to do. But we'd lost him just last year.

When I turned toward Lisa to tell her how much I thought he took after grandpa, she was gone. I looked at the door just in time to catch sight of her back as she left the restaurant. I turned my attention to the infant and wondered for the millionth time if I'd finally lost my best friend. The anxiety of losing her and my grandpa, all within a year of each other, began to take over, but when I stared at the baby, something loosened inside me. I had no idea how I was going to manage an infant, but having him, even though I'd just found out about him, seemed to fill the holes that had been left in my heart.

I sat staring at him for what had to have been thirty minutes. Finally, a server came over and put her hand on my shoulder. "I accidentally heard some of your conversation. Do you need some help with him?"

I burst out laughing, which caused the sleeping baby to jerk and me to immediately tense. "I have no idea what I'm doing," I said, and the lady chuckled.

"If it helps any, none of us really do."

I glanced up at her, willing my tears not to flow. "But at least you had some prior warning."

The lady sighed. "I'll tell you what, I'll go through the stuff your lady friend left here, and we'll make sure you have everything you need. I've had three myself, and the youngest is three, so I know the drill."

Without looking up from the little one, I asked, "Won't you get in trouble?"

"I doubt it. I'm Catherine, I own the place, and it's unlikely my staff will have the nerve to challenge me."

She smiled when I met her gaze, and walked over, starting to go through Lisa's things. "Looks like you've got what you need. Do you have anyone you can call?"

I immediately thought of my mom. Over Christmas, I'd come out to my parents as bisexual with a preference for men, and it had gone spectacularly bad. My grandpa had known, but he'd never told them. Unfortunately, I assumed he had. Well, you can imagine what the pastor of a mega Southern Baptist church's reactions were.

My grandpa got custody of me when I was a preteen. My dad hit me so hard once, he broke my arm. I still don't remember what stupid infraction I'd committed. I just remember being picked up from the Emergency Room by my grandpa, and after that, I never lived with my parents again.

On Christmas night, when I made a comment about dating a guy, my dad's expression looked a whole lot like the one I remembered the night he broke my arm. He was bigger than I was, even though I'd just turned nineteen. I stood up and walked out of my parents' house. Luckily, he didn't strike me that time, but he hadn't spoken to me since.

"My aunt will probably help. I just need to call her. Can you hold him for a moment?" I asked.

The lady's face beamed. Not for the first time, I wondered what it was about babies and puppies that inspired such a response from the female of the species.

Catherine took him from me, and gently rocked him in her arms. The experience of child-rearing struck me as I watched her with him. For what must have been the hundredth time since Lisa told me I was a dad, I felt completely out of my element. What the hell was I going to do?

The spell broke when she looked up at me, so I pulled my phone out of my pocket and immediately called Aunt Doris. She was the closest thing to a mom I had. She'd moved in with Grandpa and me after her divorce. Just after I'd moved in with him.

"Aunt Doris," I said.

"Oh, hi, honey," she replied immediately. "This is unexpected."

"Yeah," I said, trying to find the words to explain to her what was happening. "Um, are you home?"

She hesitated. "Baby, what's wrong?" she asked. Luckily all the maternal instincts my own mom never had, Aunt Doris seemed to have in spades. Too bad she didn't have any kids of her own to share those instincts.

"Well, um..." I glanced at the baby and then at the server as I tried to figure out how I was going to explain things.

"Trevor, spit it out, sweetie. You're scaring me."

"I have a baby," I finally blurted out. "Lisa and I had a baby."

Aunt Doris was our family's carefree, happy, eccentric member who honestly believed love cured all. As I should've expected, she squealed at the news. "I'm a great aunt!" she exclaimed loud enough that the server still standing next to me smiled.

"Yeah," I said, the tears I'd managed to hold in until that point slipping down my face. "But Lisa left. She said she can't take care of him."

"Oh, baby," my aunt said. "You bring him over here, and we'll figure this out. And don't you worry about a thing 'cause I'm going to be the best great aunt that's ever been born."

Her optimism struck me squarely in the chest, and I couldn't resist letting out a sob of relief. I knew she was right. Aunt Doris had my back.

Peter

Devastation. That's what I felt.

Losing Martin because of my own stupidity was something that would always hurt. Knowing my mother was the culprit behind all the shit, well, that was more than I could handle. Moving was the only thing that made sense. I couldn't trust my mother ever again. At least not with the men in my life.

I know her hostility toward Martin was caused by the tumor, but still, it was more than I'd ever be able to forgive her for.

I'd tried dating again since Martin, but unfortunately, no one seemed to fit me. I already knew I was screwed up because I tended to compare every man I dated to him.

I know! If I'd listened to him, believed him, and confronted my mom like the mature man I was supposed to be, I'd be married to him right now.

Luckily, I'd been recruited by and accepted a job at Mr. Howard's construction company. That was where I met his son Joshua, otherwise, I wouldn't have a single friend in Atlanta. Joshua and I tried to date, but when his dad caught us behind their pool house, he fired me. Despite that, Joshua an1d I remained friends.

"What are you getting?" Joshua asked me as we sat by the window.

"I'm not really that hungry," I replied. "Wanna split a Rueben?"

"Sure."

I searched the area to see what was keeping the server. Something on the other side of the restaurant seemed to be holding her attention. I almost got up to get her when I saw a young woman walk out, leaving her infant in the arms of a small, but handsome young man.

I assumed he must be the dad, but the poor guy's facial expression looked like he'd just been hit by a truck.

Our server stood next to him, apparently trying to console him.

Eventually, she took the baby, and he picked up his phone. By then, Joshua and I, as well as most of the other patrons in the place, were glued to the events unfolding before us.

Within moments, the young man hung up his phone, took the baby back, put the little one in the baby carrier, and disappeared out the door. Joshua and I watched as he left in what must have been an Uber or Lyft. I couldn't help but wonder what kind of trouble the driver would get into if they got pulled over, and the baby wasn't properly strapped in.

Drama over, the server came to our table.

"That looked interesting," Joshua said.

The woman shook her head with a sad expression on her face. "Poor guy has no idea what he's in for. I can't imagine what it must be like to be single, footloose, young, and free one minute, then saddled with a little one the next."

"Wow, that's what happened?" I asked.

The woman continued to look sad, she closed her eyes for a moment before gathering herself together.

She didn't answer my question. Instead, she asked, "What can I do for you, boys?"

The rest of the meal went off as normal. Joshua complained about his dad but loved the work he was doing.

"When are you going to leave and get a job with someone who appreciates you?" I asked for the hundredth time.

He shrugged. "I don't know, Peter. I don't really wanna go for my MBA, and he does pay me the same as I'd make almost anywhere else. Besides, I like construction. Would you recommend I go to work for his competition?"

We both laughed at that. "Your father would literally murder you!"

"Uh-huh, so for now, I'm stuck with him."

"So, I have some good news, I'm getting a new project. Our firm has a new contract with a big international company building contemporary buildings in a steampunk style."

"Cool, and weird. Why Atlanta?" he asked.

"Just where he wants to try his new brand, and I think he liked some of my designs from when I worked in Texas. You should come to work for us," I said, and he just shook his head.

"You know that would be another easy way for me to find myself at the bottom of some river wearing concrete shoes."

I chuckled, but I was never entirely sure whether Joshua was joking or not.

Trevor

Had it not been for Aunt Doris, I don't know how the little man and I would've gotten by. I realized after we got in the Lyft that I hadn't even asked Lisa the baby's name. How does someone forget to ask that?

I tried to reach Lisa again, but no surprise, she didn't answer. I sent her a text instead.

What's his name?

She texted back moments later.

It's on his birth certificate in the baby bag. I named him Luka, after your grandpa.

I had to wipe away the tears again after learning his name. Lisa might have abandoned us, but she still knew how to be nurturing even when she was hurting.

I texted back.

You need to come back and help us out. We can figure it out.

But I got no response.

When little Luka and I arrived at my family home, Aunt Doris was sitting on the porch, apparently waiting for us. She came out to the car, and the moment I got out, she pulled me into a hug. "Baby, we will get through this, don't you fret, OK?"

Of course, the tears streamed down my face again. "Aunt Doris, what am I going to do?"

She patted my head like I was ten years old again. "What every parent has ever done. Stay up late, get up early, change poopy diapers, and fall in love with this little man."

I smiled, in spite of myself, and turned around, pulling the baby carrier out of the car while she grabbed the baby bag.

As we walked up toward the house, a thought struck me. I sure as hell hoped she meant *us* 'cause I was already scared shitless, and I hadn't thought about the poopy diapers until that moment.

***

I knew raising a baby would change everything. Luckily, I finished my bachelor's degree a semester early and I thanked God in heaven for the advanced classes I took in high school. I'd initially thought I'd spend this final semester of school enjoying a break before starting law school.

I couldn't imagine how I'd ever go to law school now that Luka was going to take so much of my and Aunt Doris's time.

At Aunt Doris's suggestion, I gave notice on my tiny apartment that was close to school and moved back in with her. Luckily, Grandpa had left me a small trust account, but I wasn't technically supposed to be able to use the money until I graduated. It was Grandpa's way of paying for my graduate studies. Once I told the attorney, who was a trustee, that I had a new baby, he agreed to monthly payments to help with expenses at least until I could show him the degree.

The monthly stipend far from covered all our expenses, so I had to get a part-time job. The law firm I did my internship with last summer didn't have anything I could do, but they told me the private investigator company they worked with was looking for someone.

I knew beggars couldn't be choosers. So with their referral, I went to the investigator's office and was hired on the spot. Luckily, I quickly discovered how much I liked that side of the business. It was mostly research, which I'd always been good at. But there was also the occasional dramatic event we got to be part of, involving cheating spouses or locating someone who'd skipped out on their child support payments.

The best part was, when I was doing research, I could work from home, which meant most of the time I could take care of Luka and not be too much of a burden on Aunt Doris.

Peter

"Mom, seriously, stop calling me so much! I told you I'm not seeing anyone right now. No, you're right, I probably wouldn't let you meet them even if I did. We've discussed this. You broke my fiancé and me up, and no, it wasn't just because you had a tumor... Mom, it doesn't matter now, I'm sorry, I have to go."

I'd gotten used to these phone conversations. I ended up arguing with her at least once a week since I started talking to her again. She wanted to blame everything on the tumor, so I'd forgive her and let things go back to the way they were before. But truth be told, I didn't think I'd ever forgive her for taking Martin away from me. No amount of apologizing would ever change that.

"Wait, honey!" she pleaded over the phone. "I don't know what to do to make this right. It's been two years. I miss you, and of course, I want to meet your boyfriends. You shouldn't keep them from me. I went to Dr. Lacie's last week, and she confirmed the tumor is gone. I won't be that way again. I promise."

I sighed into the phone. "Mom, I'm not dating. I swear to God."

This seemed to appease her, at least for the moment. I wanted to tell her that she could probably just give up on me ever dating again, but I was beginning to feel bad about how I was treating her. I'd talked to Dr. Lacie myself, and she confirmed that most of what Mom had said to Martin was because of the tumor. Hell, even *Madam Secretary* had a whole episode about it when President Dalton had the same tumor Mom did. She'd called me the night the episode aired, all excited because she was sure that the show's endorsement would help me forgive and forget.

I wish it had. I often regretted that I couldn't get past it. That Christmas, I lost not only my fiancé, I lost my mom as well. I missed our relationship and how easy it used to be for us to talk. I couldn't imagine a time when my anger wouldn't stop that from happening again.

"Mom, I'm sorry, but I have to get back to work. I have a deadline, remember?"

"OK, honey, but I would really like to see you soon. When are you coming back to Austin?"

Again, a bone of contention between us. I'd been recruited by a firm in Austin for a potential job over the summer and happened to run into Martin. I'd gone to his house to beg him to give me another chance, but he made it clear he'd moved on. That's when the walls really went up between Mom and I. She'd been trying to tear them back down ever since.

The fact that I skipped Thanksgiving and Christmas this year really put her in a bad place. My aunt called to tell me and to try to manipulate me into coming home.

"You can't blame your mother for having a brain tumor, Peter," my aunt said, frustration oozing through the phone connection.

"I don't blame her for having a brain tumor, Auntie. I blame her for intentionally breaking my relationship up."

"She didn't do it intentionally. It was the tumor."

"No, she didn't like him. The tumor gave her an excuse to spew venom, but it was her dislike that split us up."

We continued to argue until my aunt hung up on me.

C'est la vie, I wouldn't be manipulated or controlled. Mom created this mess because she did what she did. The tumor was just part of the problem. She'd always hated my dates, always walked a fine line between humor and being hateful. She was jealous, and I knew it, and yet I still hadn't believed Martin when he'd confided in me about how she'd treated him.

The reminder hit home, and with great effort, I tried hard not to be disrespectful. "Mom, I don't know. I've got to go, sorry. Love you." I hung up without a response, knowing there would've been at least another fifteen minutes of manipulative banter if I hadn't.

I put my head down on my desk and willed myself to cry. I wasn't good at emotional stuff. As a gay man, I should've been able to at least shed a tear, but as horrible as everything was, I only cried once, and that was when I'd found out Mom did everything Martin said she'd done. I cried more from anger than hurt, though. Anger at myself more than anything.

Since then, I'd been numb. I couldn't feel much of anything other than anxious regret, and although I thought a good crying jag would help, I didn't have it in me to pull it off.

Trevor

When I looked up from my desk and stared into the lobby, I immediately spotted the short woman who was my next client. She couldn't have been more than five foot four, but she wore heels and expensive clothing, which made her appear significantly taller than she was.

I went out to the front desk instead of paging the secretary and called her name, "Mrs. Reed?"

The woman smiled at me and followed me back.

"So how can I help you, Mrs. Reed?" I asked.

The woman stared at me a moment, then shook her head. "I made a real bad mess of things with my son, and I need someone to help me make it better."

I stared at her for a moment and waited for her to continue. When she didn't, I responded, "I'm not sure how we can help."

"Well, to start, you can follow my son and tell me if he has a boyfriend that he isn't telling me about."

I took in the feisty woman in front of me and immediately wished she'd talked to someone besides me. I simply wouldn't play a part in harassing her gay son because she had some religious problem.

"Ma'am, before we go any further, you should know I'm bisexual myself. I personally won't be able to get involved with a witch hunt or anything that would hurt your son. However, if you wait here, I'll go get someone else who might be able to help."

The woman's face registered shock, then grief. "No, I'm not a religious zealot! Oh, dear God, you thought I was going to chase my son down to preach hate to him? For goodness sake, I was a PFLAG president for four years!"

I sat back down and shook my head. "I'm sorry, I don't understand then. Why don't you just ask your son if he's dating anyone?"

The lady leaned back in her chair with a sigh. She explained how she'd treated her son's ex-fiancé and how she had a tumor that caused her to cross the line with him. "It's like I didn't have control over my own nasty mouth!" she said as tears threatened to flow.

"Can I level with you, Mrs..."

"Call me Matilda," she interrupted me, "and please do."

"If I were your son and after what you told me you'd done to his ex, if I found out you had a private investigator stalking me, that would pretty much end any contact I'd have with you."

Her tears did flow then. She picked up a tissue and dabbed her eyes.

"I know... my sister told me the same thing, but I don't know what else to do. I flew all the way out here hoping to see him, but he got mad at me for putting pressure on him and asked me to stay at a hotel. He's already mad enough not to speak to me."

I sighed and leaned back in my chair, too. I knew I should probably be trying to get this woman's business, but in good conscience, I couldn't allow her to screw this up worse than it already was.

"I'll tell you what, is there any chance his ex-fiancé would be willing to listen to you if you apologized directly to him?"

She shook her head. "No, I was the devil himself to that boy. He'd probably call the police if I tried to talk to him."

"Do you still want to keep them apart?" I asked.

She shook her head. "No, I wish I could go back and undo what I've done."

"Well, can I suggest you leave your son in peace and pursue that direction instead? I can't say it'll help, but it might help your son to see you're trying."

Mrs. Reed considered what I said for a long moment. "I think you're right. I think that's the way I should approach this."

I smiled and patted the hand she'd placed on my desk.

"I wish you all the luck," I said as I escorted her out.

Peter

I was so pissed off when I'd found out my mother had come to Atlanta, to force her way into my life again. The truth is, I'd almost buckled and was getting ready to go home for a weekend visit when I got the call. Hell, she hadn't even waited.

I'd been more than a little put out and told her to stay at a hotel around the corner from where I lived. I probably should've sucked up my pride and let her stay with me, but I just couldn't.

I didn't hear from her the next day, which worried me. My mom wasn't known for letting things go that easily. That evening, I called her and asked what she was up to. She hemmed and hawed enough that I knew she was indeed up to something and that it would probably be bad for me.

I asked her if she wanted to meet for dinner, but she declined saying she was leaving to return home early in the morning. Now I was seriously concerned.

"Mom, what are you up to?"

"Honey, I have no idea what you mean. I came to see you, but you didn't want to see me, so now I'm going home."

"Mother, you know I love you. You also know I know you better than most people. When you decline the chance to meet me for dinner and pound your agenda into me, I'm fully aware there's something else going on."

My mom huffed into the phone, then blew me off. "Honey, I'm right in the middle of packing. I'll phone you when I get back home." Then she hung up.

Shit, I should've swallowed my pride and let her stay with me. There's absolutely no telling what she'd gotten me into. All I could do at this point was pray it didn't blow up like Martin had.

Trevor

A week after Mrs. Reed visited me, I got a phone call from her. Luka was wailing in the background, so I had to put her on hold and find Aunt Doris before I could speak.

When I got back to the phone, she was chuckling. "I remember those days," she said. "Does your wife work at home, too?"

I smiled. "No, it's just me and my Aunt Doris. How can I help you, Mrs. Reed?"

The lady sighed so heavily I could hear her exasperation through the phone. "Well, I tried to take your advice to track Martin down, but apparently he's moved to Florida, and no one will tell me which part. I even went to his parents' house and was lucky they didn't call the police on me. I told you, I really screwed the pooch on this one. I have no idea what to do next."

I thought for a few moments about what she'd said. "I'll be honest, Mrs. Reed, if things are that tense, you might not want to pursue this any further. I didn't realize things were that bad."

She sighed again. "No, you were right. This is the way I should make amends. I should've gone to the boy right after I had surgery and apologized for how I'd acted. 'We need to clean up our own mistakes,' that's what my father used to tell me over and over. I preached the same thing to Peter growing up, so it's time I face the music and make amends for my behavior. Even if it's difficult."

I was reticent about helping her go any further, not knowing how this would turn out. I could tell Mrs. Reed was a force to be reckoned with, but if the guy's parents threatened to have her arrested, there must still be a lot of bad blood there.

"I'll tell you what," I replied. "I'll send over a contract for you to review regarding how my company handles different scenarios and detailing our services. If you agree, I'll check on where this Martin is currently located. I'll need you to fill out what you know about him and send me that info as well. Once I locate him, we can come up with a plan from there."

Mrs. Reed seemed satisfied with my suggestion. So much so that I received the signed paperwork back within a few hours of emailing it to her.

Martin Williams wasn't difficult to find. He'd become a well-respected food critic in Fort Lauderdale. I was feeling optimistic about a resolution for Mrs. Reed until I found a wedding announcement for him and one Elian Whitman. Nevertheless, I jotted down his contact information on one of the company's many forms and contacted Mrs. Reed about what I found.

Matilda was disappointed that Martin was engaged.

"Oh, honey, I was hoping I could clean up my mistakes and give Peter and Martin another chance." She sighed so heavily, I almost chuckled. The woman was one hundred percent Southern belle.

"I'm gonna ponder this a little further and see how I wanted to proceed," she said before hanging up.

Not surprisingly, I got another phone call from her the following day, telling me she wanted to track Martin down and apologize.

"I'm not sure that's a good idea," I told her honestly.

"It isn't. The boy is sure to still be spitting mad at me, but as I said, I need to clean this up once and for all."

"Mrs. Reed, I'm not sure how much money you want to spend on this, but I'd be much more comfortable if you'd let me accompany you if you plan to meet him in person."

"I was going to ask if you'd consider going with me."

"Let me speak to my supervisors and get their permission. If they agree, I'll send over the additional paperwork."

When I spoke to my supervisor, she laughed her butt off. "You're going to chase down a guy this woman monster-in-lawed so she can apologize?"

I had to laugh, too. "Apparently, I am. To be honest, I'm afraid to let her go by herself. I have no idea how all this will work out in the end."

My supervisor gave her blessing, and when Mrs. Reed agreed to the costs, we planned for me to meet her in Fort Lauderdale the following weekend. She decided she'd rather I didn't contact Martin first because she didn't want him to refuse to see her until she was at his door.

I went through back channels to find out where his office was while thinking that would probably be the least likely place for an eruption to take place. I went ahead and set up an appointment with him for the Friday after we arrived. It was easy to pretend to be a restaurant owner, and I secretly hoped the pretense wouldn't lead to more of an upset.

***

After I met Mrs. Reed at the airport, I escorted her to the hotel I'd rented for the both of us, close to Martin's work. We dropped off our luggage and met at the hotel's restaurant to discuss strategy.

"I've set up an appointment at Martin's workplace. It's in my name, so he doesn't know it's you he's meeting." Mrs. Reed looked nonplused. "Are you sure you want to go through with this?" I asked.

"Yes, I'm here now. It's good to have a chance to apologize. Even though I'm scared half out of my wits."

I chuckled. "Well, there isn't much he'll be able to do. Hopefully, meeting you at work will make it a bit less dramatic. That's why I set it up this way."

She sighed again and patted my hand. "I'm so thankful for what you've done to make this possible. I can't imagine how I'd have worked it all out on my own."

I smiled. "Don't thank me yet. This is still set up to be a total disaster. I have every expectation it will blow up in our faces, but at least you'll have me by your side if it does."

Mrs. Reed smiled again. "I ordered a bottle of Champagne as well as a bottle of Jack to be dropped off at my hotel room. Regardless of how this works out, I'm prepared for the evening."

"I have to admit, you are quite a character," I told her, chuckling. "If you don't mind me asking, I'm curious how all this went down between you two."

Mrs. Reed leaned back in the odd-shaped chair and let out one of the sighs I'd come to expect from her.

"Well, I admit I didn't really like Martin when I first met him. He's attractive enough, but I always thought my boy would marry, well, someone different."

I cocked an eyebrow at her, which made her laugh. "I know, I was being petty. I think all parents get caught up in whether or not their kid's companions are good enough for them, but when most parents keep their mouths shut, I didn't. I remember how angry I got when Peter announced he and Martin were getting married. I should've been over the moon, but all I could think of was that he was marrying some low-life trailer trash, and I needed to stop it if I could. The more I thought about it, the angrier I got. In fact, I can say that was the angriest I've ever been. Christmas Eve was the climax as I hadn't seen the two of them since they'd come over to announce their engagement. So, when Peter left the room, I laid into the boy."

The woman wiped a tear from her eye. "I'm going to be honest, I said some of the worst, most hateful things that have ever come out of my mouth. None of it's worth repeating, but I'll be the first to tell you even I think it was unforgivable. Finally, Martin had enough of it. He went and sat in the main room where I couldn't be alone with him. I remember even that set me off to the point that I could've killed him."

Her expression became serious. "I mean, seriously, I could've really killed him. As they were leaving, I shot him as many hateful looks as possible, at least when Peter wasn't looking. Even in that state, I knew I needed to keep Peter out of the loop with my plans to get rid of the vagrant. So, I wasn't surprised, in fact, I was elated the next day to find out Peter and Martin had split up. When I hung up the phone with Peter, I even danced around the room. At least until my head almost split open with pain. That's the last thing I remember until I woke up in a hospital bed several weeks later. When I finally came to and could function like a real human being, the rift between Peter and Martin must have been too great for him to cross. I never heard what he did or if he even tried to contact Martin, and I was too embarrassed to do anything about it myself. I didn't recover quickly, in fact, it took months for me to regain even the basic of functions. Now looking back, I wish I'd gone to see Martin as soon as I could walk or at least when I was released to drive, and apologized. But, as you know, I didn't. So here we sit now."

I was completely caught up in the story. "That's sad and painful to listen to, Mrs. Reed. I can't imagine what it was like for any of you."

"Excruciating for all parties I can assure you, but that doesn't let me off the hook. In fact, I totally understand why everyone would hate me, but, Mr. Kovachich, did I say your name correctly?" I nodded to encourage her to go on with her story.

"I need my son back. I feel like I've lost so much from that tumor. I'm glad... I really am, that I was lucky enough that my tumor wasn't malignant or that it hasn't returned, which the doctors told me it could and probably would. I almost... sometimes I wish it'd taken me. I don't know what I'm going to do without Peter in my life."

The tears flowed freely. I could tell the older woman across from me was anguished from the events that happened between her and her son.

"Can I offer some advice?" I asked.

She nodded but didn't respond.

"If you go into that office today and allow yourself to be as vulnerable as you've been with me, I'm sure Martin will see your sincerity. I fear your confidence and straight-forward manner might be something that would keep him from listening to you. As you are right now, seeing how you hurt for what the tumor caused you to do, that is what he needs to see and hear."

She nodded again, then stood to excuse herself. "I'm going to go lie down for a bit and get my wits about me." We arranged a time to meet, and she left me where I sat.

I stayed in the restaurant for a long time and thought about how I'd feel if my mom, or my dad, for that matter, ever worked this hard to make up for something they'd done. The thought almost amused me. I couldn't imagine either of them cared enough about me to even try. Hell, even after my dad broke my arm, he never apologized or even looked remorseful. I could only imagine how her son must have felt, but he had to also know this woman would do anything for him. Hell, she *was* doing something big for him in coming here. I just hoped he ended up seeing it for the generosity it was.

***

The meeting between Martin and Mrs. Reed went better than I expected.

When we first walked in, Martin was angry. "I'm calling security," he said. His boss even came over to intervene.

Matilda burst into tears. "You've every right, Martin, what I said to you was inexcusable. We can leave, I just wanted you to know how sorry I am."

When we turned, he said, "No, stop, if you're really sorry, I've got a moment."

Mrs. Reed had taken my advice and allowed herself to be vulnerable and sincere in her apology.

She basically explained to Martin what she'd told me in the restaurant and before we left, Martin hugged her.

Throughout their exchange, tears slipped down the older woman's face. She told him about how the tumor had taken over. She also admitted she didn't like him, but that had nothing to do with him and everything to do with her being overprotective of Peter.

When I glanced over at the man we'd come so far to meet, I noticed a tear had slipped down his face as well.

"You'll never understand how much this means to me," he told her. "I've agonized about how all that happened, internalized it, and I've even pushed people away who love me and who I love in return."

She smiled. "I see you're getting married."

His face lit up, and I could see love written all over him. Apparently, so could Mrs. Reed.

"I am, he's a restaurateur. He's a good guy, too," Martin replied.

After a bit more conversation, Mrs. Reed stood and drew Martin into her arms. "I wish you and your new man all the best, Martin. Despite what I said to you, you are a wonderful man."

He smiled at her. "That the best wedding gift I've gotten thus far. Believe it or not, this will help a lot in letting go of the past so I can move on."

Mrs. Reed wanted to see a picture of Elian. I wanted to protest, but when she saw his picture, she smiled. "He's really a looker, huh?" she said.

Martin had a goofy grin on his face at that point, which clearly showed just how much he was in love with the guy. If I'd been brave enough, and this hadn't been a moment between Mrs. Reed and Martin, I'd have wanted to know whether he'd felt that same kind of giddy love for Mrs. Reed's son. Unfortunately, it wasn't my place to ask such things, so I kept those thoughts and questions to myself.

As we rode back to the hotel, I let Mrs. Reed lean over, giving her a side hug as she cried all the way back. Before we got out of the cab, she said, "He really loves that new guy, you can tell. I guess I couldn't see that kind of love in him before because of the tumor, but I don't think I'll ever forgive myself for taking that away from Peter."

"Oh, don't be upset. If your Peter found a love like him once, I'm sure he'll find it again. Just give him space and time."

We got out of the taxi and went to sit in the lobby before we retired to our separate rooms.

I found a vending machine, bought us both a soda, and went over to sit next to her. "I only have one last bit of advice for you," I said. "You need to let Peter know what you've done and the sooner the better. In fact, I suggest you call him tonight before he finds out from someone else. If I were your son, I'd take this as meddling, and I'd be irate, so you should plan on that being a possible response. But in the long run, what you did today was really awesome." I could feel myself becoming emotional after the day's events. "It was healing for him, and I think for you, too, and believe it or not, it touched me pretty deeply as well, so even if Peter gets really angry with you, remember you did the right thing, OK?"

She looked at me again and patted my hand. "Thank you, Trevor." That was the first time she'd used my first name.

"You are the reason I got through this, and I'll never forget your support. Now, enough of all this, I want to hear about that little person I heard that time I called you."

I must have gotten googly eyes because she laughed at me. "You got it bad, son," she replied. "How old is the little one?"

I smiled in spite of myself. Since Lisa had left Luka with me, I'd steadily fallen deeper and deeper in love with my son.

"He's growing so fast," I told her. "I know I'm biased, but I think he's the most beautiful baby that's ever lived. His eyes are so blue Frank Sinatra has nothing on him, and I'm holding out that he's going to be a crooner himself. If you heard the lungs on that boy, you'd know what I mean. He's like his mom in that way, no patience whatsoever."

"So, are you and his mother still close?"

I must've shown my sadness because Mrs. Reed patted my hand. "Broke up, huh?"

"No, not really. His mom and I were best friends, and little Luka is the result of a night of binge drinking and bad decisions. When she found out she was pregnant, she shut me out of her life. I only saw her for a moment while she dropped Luka off for me to take custody."

"You miss her?" she asked.

"Yeah, we were really close, and I regret that she isn't getting to watch Luka grow up."

"When Peter's dad died, I felt so betrayed. Every day I thought how much he was missing with Peter. But whether the mom comes back or not, that baby will know you love him, and that's good enough, even on the hard days. Don't forget that."

I saw the sincerity in Mrs. Reed's face. She loved her son and must've been a great mother. I wished I could meet her son just to find out what kind of person he was. If this woman across from me was any indication, he'd be one of the good ones.

Emotionally, I think both Mrs. Reed and I were too tired to keep up a conversation for much longer. "I think it's time you go crack that bottle of Champagne," I told her, and she winked at me.

"I think I'm going to do just that. Do you want to join me?" she asked.

"No, I'm beat, and I have to be on a flight out by five o'clock in the morning. When I get home, I'll be on Luka duty again, which means I've got to be on my toes."

Mrs. Reed laughed. "You better take advantage of a full night's sleep while you can!"

We parted company, and Mrs. Reed gave me a hug before turning in. It would likely be the last time I'd see her, as she was leaving on a later flight than me. I was also sure the moment I put my head on a pillow, I'd be done until morning.

As I stripped and got into bed, I realized it was still only six o'clock, I chuckled at how much my life had changed since Luka came into it.

Aunt Doris said Luka was probably messed up by Lisa's leaving. Babies can hear their mom's heartbeats while developing, and studies have shown that a baby can recognize their mom compared to others. We both agreed, Luka was going through separation anxiety. Unfortunately, knowing that didn't mean the lack of sleep didn't weigh on us both.

On one occasion, Aunt Doris proposed we tell my mom about Luka if for no other reason than to have another person to come help with him during the night. Then we both looked at each other and shook our heads at the same time.

Aunt Doris chuckled. "No, that would be worse, then we'd have to hear both your mom and Luka yelling at us."

She was right. We'd agreed when Luka first arrived that until he got settled, it was best not to tell my parents about him. Besides, they didn't want to be around me anyway, and I sure as hell didn't want to deal with a newborn *and* the childishness of my parents.

So, the two of us did what we could to endure raising a very grumpy infant who clearly missed his mama.

***

I woke up earlier than my alarm the next morning, and my heart ached to get my son back in my arms. I rushed home from the airport just in time to rescue Aunt Doris from what appeared to be a mental breakdown.

"He didn't sleep, huh?"

"Not even a wink," she sighed. "Glad you're home." She kissed me on the temple, then disappeared to her room. "You've got Luka duty for the rest of the weekend," she said as she climbed the stairs.

Luka settled almost immediately after I picked him up and fed him his morning bottle. I was so thankful I'd gotten a full night's sleep but felt really bad for Aunt Doris. As Luka dozed in my arms, I couldn't help but stare at him. Would there be a time when he refused to talk to me like Mrs. Reed's son refused to talk to her?

It was, then I realized if I was ever in that same situation, I'd go to the ends of the earth to clean up anything I'd done and to reconcile with him, just as she'd done for Peter. Even in the short time I'd had him, Luka meant everything to me, and I'd do anything in my power to keep him happy and healthy.

***

On Monday morning, I planned to spend the day working from home. Aunt Doris hadn't recovered from my night in Fort Lauderdale, so I still had Luka duty. Unfortunately, it all went downhill when, at eight o'clock, the office called telling me I had an angry customer in my office, and I needed to deal with him.

I couldn't imagine who was angry enough with me to turn up at my office, demanding to see me. Heck, the only cases besides Mrs. Reed's was a missing person's case my boss was working on, and a divorce case, but since both the husband and wife had been cheating on each other, they'd decided to split mutually. Unless the husband had decided he wasn't happy after all, I had no idea who'd be at my office creating such a ruckus.

I agreed to be in the office by nine, but I told my boss I had to bring Luka with me since I couldn't get a sitter at such short notice. Luckily, my boss had fallen for little Luka and quickly agreed to baby duty while I navigated all the drama.

I arrived a couple minutes after nine, having had to rush through a shower, dress like a professional, dress Luka, pack him and the baby carrier into the taxi because Grandpa's car wouldn't start, unpack him and get into the office. Geez, hauling a baby around was a hell of a lot of work. No wonder most new moms appear to be ready to commit *hara-kiri* at any moment.

When I got to the office, the secretary met me and took Luka off my hands. "You need to go right in. The guy refuses to leave until you show up."

"Really?" I asked. "Who is he?"

She just shrugged and began playing with Luka, totally ignoring me.

I just sighed. I'd gotten used to the expression that came over some people's faces when I walked into a room with Luka. It was almost like I completely disappeared.

I started turning toward the waiting room when the secretary looked up at me like she'd just remembered she was at work. "Oh, I put him in your office. He was too irate to be out in the lobby where other clients might hear him."

I just shook my head, not knowing who the hell could've been that angry. I wondered if maybe I needed to have some backup with me before going in.

I stopped at my supervisor's office and asked if I needed backup. Linda, my supervisor, just smiled. "No, you'll be fine, but he's plenty mad."

"Who is he?" I asked.

"Not exactly sure, but he's really nice to look at."

I shook my head. "Seriously, I'm not gonna get backup because he's hot?" I asked, and she chuckled.

I stomped toward my office, keen to get this over and done with. The sooner I was done, the sooner I could get Luka back home and actually get some work done. Hell, I got paid mostly on commission, and I had expenses coming up. Seriously, after traipsing all over Florida to help Mrs. Reed, I was way behind on the work I needed to finish up my other cases.

I stopped at my office door, drew in a deep breath, and walked in.

The man stood up slowly. He was obviously still angry, but now I understood what Linda meant. The man was drop-dead gorgeous. Tall, with bronze skin, perfectly beautiful hair, and even with the scowl, he could've been on the cover of a magazine.

"Can I help you, sir?" I asked, trying to keep my tongue from falling out of my mouth.

"Are you the little instigator who dragged my mother down to Florida to stir up shit that needed to be left the fuck alone?"

I was totally taken aback. "Excuse me?"

"You, I'm asking you. Did you just come back from Florida, where you took my mother, Matilda Reed, to Fort Lauderdale to get all up in the middle of a shit storm with my ex?"

Before I could get all the way into the office, I heard the all too familiar wail of my son.

"Hold that thought," I said as I turned to go pick Luka up from whoever had offended his sensibilities. That particular wail was his most angry one, and if anyone but me tried to appease him, it'd just pissed him off more.

I rushed over to where the secretary was handing Luka off to Linda. Both women's faces were filled with terror, and I laughed as I took him from them. "Y'all look like you're about to be attacked by a lion or something."

"Wow, he has some lungs!" Linda said.

"Oh, you have no idea," I replied. "I'll just take him with me. The guy is Mrs. Reed's son. Maybe holding a baby will prevent me from getting busted in the face."

Linda yelled out behind me. "Ask him if he's single!" Since Luka was still wailing, I just pretended like I didn't hear her.

"I'm so sorry, I had to bring my son in with me. Today's a work from home day," I said as I walked into the office and threw the baby bag onto my desk. I was rummaging through it looking for Luka's bottle, praying he wouldn't get so worked up he wouldn't take it. I hadn't paid attention to Peter since coming back in.

Peter

Mom had called me Friday night and told me what she'd done. I was mortified. It was bad enough that Martin had endured everything he had from us, but it was so much worse that we kept popping back up in his life like a bad penny. No, worse, a bad penny with a venereal disease.

I yelled at my mom on the phone, hung up on her, then called her back the next day when she said she'd be back home and yelled at her again. Uncharacteristically, she stoically allowed me to blow off steam instead of chastising me about respecting my elders or not talking to her with respect.

Of course, that made my anger that much worse. Damn, if she didn't *know* I was correct, what the hell was she thinking?

When I'd finished blowing my top, she simply said, "I love you, honey, and I'm sorry you're upset. Martin took it well if you want to know. Call me when you're ready to talk."

I said goodbye as quickly as I could because I knew I wouldn't be able to hold back the stream of curse words that were ready to erupt from my mouth. No matter how composed she was, I knew if I'd said what I needed to say, she'd be on a plane to Atlanta with the sole intention of whipping my ass. Which she'd only done once in my life, and that was when I shot my neighbor's cat with a BB gun I'd gotten for Christmas.

After hanging up, the rage still filled me. Anger consumed me and screamed for release. I kept rehashing the crap that happened two years before, when my mom literally ended my relationship with the only man I'd ever loved and probably ever would love. That, combined with my own stupidity at not listening to him and taking her side when I *knew* he was telling the truth. Of course, Martin told the truth... he'd always told me the truth, it's the very thing that made me fall in love with him in the first place.

When Martin called on Sunday afternoon, I was mortified as well as angry. He told me how well it had gone and how thankful he was that Matilda had gone to all that trouble to apologize. "It's just the healing I needed," he admitted.

I could tell by his voice something had shifted in him since we'd spoken last summer, when I showed up at his parents' place trying to get him back. I'd been mourning his loss since then, and the anger with my mom only magnified from there.

"I'm getting married, Peter," he said, and I thought my world was going to crumble from under me. "I had a hard time letting his family in, and that's because I kept waiting for the next shoe to drop. But your mom coming out here, that helped, it made it better."

My voice cracked a bit. "Is he good to you?"

I could hear in Martin's voice how much he must care about the guy. "Yeah, he's really good to me."

"I'm glad, Martin. You deserve the best."

"Peter, go easy on your mom. I spent the past two years hating her, but she really regrets what happened. With the tumor, it really wasn't her fault. I've even looked up the kind she said she had, and her behavior wasn't atypical at all."

Somehow, he ended up telling me the private investigator's name and how he'd set up some kind of ruse to get my mom into his office. Martin laughed about how it had worked, but all I could see was red.

Having the man's name was all I needed. I wished Martin all the luck in the world. After hanging up, I wrapped up all my anger at my mother, myself, and the situation with Martin, and put all my energy into finding the investigator. And by God, even if I ended up in jail for the rest of my life, I was going to give that man what he had coming.

I arrived at his office at seven the next morning, which was an hour before they opened, and waited, and stewed in my own juices until some poor woman showed up to unlock the front door. Luckily, years of training by a single mother had taught me not to put a woman by herself in a situation where she was dealing with an angry man, so I waited until more people showed up before I went in.

The lady I'd seen come in first was at the front desk.

"Hi and welcome, how can I help you?" The woman's perky morning attitude grated on me that much more.

"Where is Trevor Kovachich?" I asked.

The secretary looked at me with concern on her face.

"I'm sorry, sir. Mr. Kovachich works from home most days. I don't think he's coming in today."

"Then you call that son of a bitch and tell him to get his meddling ass down here 'cause I'm not leaving until I can see him face to face."

The woman didn't even ask me to have a seat. Instead, she excused herself, which was probably best since I was spun tight enough to explode.

When she returned, another woman was in tow, who escorted me back toward an office with minimal furniture and decor. "This is Mr. Kovachich's office," she said. "I'll call him and see if he can make it in."

Then she left and was gone for several minutes. I wondered if I was about to be escorted off the premises by some brute or even the cops, but I didn't give a damn. I was going to talk to this man if it killed me. So I could kill him!

The woman returned a few minutes later and said that Mr. Kovachich was on his way, but he wouldn't be there for at least an hour, maybe more.

"I'll wait right here until he arrives!" I said with as much venom as I could put into the words. It shocked me, but when I looked at the woman, it appeared she was trying to stifle a smile. Did she think it was funny?

That just stoked the fire in me once again. I sat for a full hour building steam before the man walked into his office. When I confronted him, he didn't act like he knew what I was talking about, so I spelled it out, all while resisting the urge to take a punch at his well-developed chin.

Before I could react, however, a loud screech sounded from somewhere behind him. The man's face paled, and he quickly ducked out of the room. When he returned, he was carrying an infant that was screaming like an Irish banshee.

The man frantically searched through a baby bag until he found a bottle. He quickly knocked the top off and stuck it into the baby's mouth. At first, the infant appeared to refuse it. But after some soft talk and cajoling, the baby accepted the bottle and snuggled into the man.

The relief on the man's face was instant. "That was his no-nonsense cry. You gotta get it under control when it first starts, or there are hours and hours... and hours of screaming. It would've been the end of any meeting if I hadn't calmed him down. Sorry, you were saying?"

When I looked at the baby who was happily sucking the bottle, then back up at the man, I realized instantly he was the one I'd seen that day months ago when his girlfriend had dumped the baby on him.

Call it a miracle, or the magic associated with a happy baby, but my anger flowed right out of me at the memory. I suddenly didn't know why I was there, and when the anger faded, exhaustion crept in to take its place.

"My mom shouldn't have hired you to do that," I finally said.

The man stared at me for a moment. "Do you have a car?" he finally asked, shocking me.

I raised an eyebrow in confusion. "Yeah, why?"

"'Cause I'm going to let you take me out to breakfast since you dragged me and this little ball of anger out so early this morning, and I'll tell you all about your mom and how everything shook out."

I stared at him, thinking maybe he was a little off, but I was curious about the details. Not only that, I was also curious about what had happened to this man since I'd seen him on that day after New Year's when he first learned he was a dad.

After several tries, we got the baby carrier secured in my little convertible's back seat.

When he said he didn't care where we ate, I, maybe a little vengefully, took us to the diner where I'd seen his girlfriend leave the baby with him.

When he noticed where we were, he blanched a little. But to his credit, he didn't complain.

We got out and walked inside. The server who'd served him that day squealed from behind the counter. "Oh My God!" she said. "I wondered if we were going to see you again." She ran over and started playing with the baby while Trevor looked on with a smile on his face. "Can I hold him?"

"Of course," he replied, and he removed the baby from the carrier and handed him to her.

At first, I waited for the little one to scream as he had before, but maybe because of his full belly, he didn't seem to mind. "He needs to be burped, though," he said to her. "So be careful you don't end up with spit-up all over you."

"Don't you worry, I've got experience with such things. Can I take him back and show him off to the other staff?"

The guy just laughed. "I'm sure they all want to meet him, huh?"

The lady appeared shy. "You've been the talk of this place since that day."

"I'm sure," he said but in good spirits. "His name's Luka. I didn't know at the time, but that's his name."

The woman replied, "Hi there, Luka. You look so much like your daddy. I bet you're stealing hearts everywhere you go."

I turned toward the guy, who cocked an eyebrow at the comment but didn't say anything.

"You two go on over there and sit down. I'm afraid it's going to be a moment before you get any service 'cause we need time to make-over this little piece of cuteness, but one of us will get to you eventually."

"Take your time," the guy said, still grinning.

We sat down at the table the woman pointed out and pretended to look at the menu. Both of us tried figuring out how to proceed with our awkward conversation. The drive over had been filled with the guy trying to keep the baby quiet. My BMW was clearly not designed for a baby, so it was difficult for him to turn and keep the bottle in the little one's mouth. That meant we hadn't really had a conversation until now.

The entire staff was behind the counter, each one crooning over the little one. The guy across from me got up, grabbed a coffee pot from the ledge behind us that the server left there when we came in, and poured himself a cup of coffee. "You want some?" he asked.

I nodded, still unsure what to say.

As he poured my coffee, he chuckled. "We might as well enjoy this 'cause I'm doubting anyone will get service as long as Luka is here."

"Why did you take my mom to Florida?" I finally asked.

"Because she hired me," he said in a matter-of-fact tone.

"But that was the worst thing you could've done. It was unethical."

The man put the coffee pot back on the ledge and sat down. This time looking me in the face.

"I'm not sure how much of this you know, but I'll start at the beginning. When your mom came to me, she was hell-bent on having me follow you to figure out why you were ignoring her." His good humor continued as he chuckled a bit at the understatement. "Knowing that was not a good thing to do, I discouraged her."

"I can thank you for that, at least."

The guy laughed out loud this time. "Oh, trust me, I know that a mom hiring a private investigator to track her son would not be the best way to make amends. Hell, I just came out to mine at Christmas."

"Shit," I replied. "Then you found out you had a baby?"

The guy looked at me, warily. "I'm going to let that comment sit for a moment until I've finished my story, then you can tell me how you knew that."

I nodded, knowing I'd given away more information than I'd meant to.

"Anyway," the guy continued, "when I found out what she'd said to your ex, I asked her why she hadn't tried to make amends with him. That's what I think put all the ideas in her head."

I could feel the anger picking up, and I tried to wrestle it back down until I could at least get the rest of the story.

"Long story short, your mother couldn't find Martin in Austin and hired my company to find where he'd gone. She said something about how your grandfather used to say that you had to clean up your own mess, or something along those lines. After we found him, she decided to go to Fort Lauderdale to make amends." The guy locked eyes with me, daring me to contradict him as he continued. "I didn't know anything about your ex or anything else for that matter, so when she told me she was bound to talk to the guy, I convinced her to hire me as her escort. At the very least, I could keep her safe while she went about it."

When he finished his story, I leaned back, exhaustion hitting me again. "I wish she hadn't gone," I said with a sigh.

"I'm sure you do, but I was there, and the whole experience was a beautiful thing to watch. Martin, your ex, was angry when he first saw her, but as she apologized, something happened between them.

Healing on both sides. It might not have been what you'd have wished, but it worked out well in the end."

"That's what Martin said," I admitted, rational thought only now sinking in for the first time since I'd talked to my mother on Friday.

"It's not any of my business, but if you'll excuse my prying, you might consider letting your mom off the hook regarding all this. At least a bit."

I narrowed my eyes at him. "You're just trying to save your skin now you don't have a baby to protect you."

He laughed. "Well, maybe, but if I'd been too scared of you, I probably wouldn't have asked you to take us out to breakfast."

Within seconds, the woman brought the baby back. "If you ever need a sitter, I could hook you up with about three of my servers."

He winked at her. "Careful, I might take you all up on that. And just so you know, it might take all three of you to watch him since he seems to have inherited his mother's stubborn disposition."

The mention of Luka's mother caused the woman's face to cloud over. I could tell she wanted to ask more, but instead, she asked in a falsely chipper voice, "So, have you decided what you're gonna have?"

"I'm having the Falcon's special," he replied.

"I'll have the same," I said.

After we'd got our eggs and other stuff on our order worked out, the woman disappeared.

"So, your turn. How did you know I found out I was a dad after coming out to my parents? Are you a private investigator as well?"

I felt my face turn red. I was going to have to confess that I'd set him up by bringing him here.

"You and your ex were here right after New Year's at the same time I was. I was with my friend, and we watched the whole ordeal go down. I didn't recognize you until you brought the baby in with you."

I could see the realization dawning on him. Why I'd chosen this place for breakfast, and he laughed out loud.

"So, you were getting me back by bringing me here?"

When he said it out loud, I felt like a total ass. "I'm afraid so."

"Touché," he replied. "Touché."

Things got awkward between us then, and neither of us knew what to say. Luckily, the food arrived, and we had a moment to collect our thoughts.

"So, what's it like to be the parent of an infant?" I asked.

He thought for a moment, then shrugged. "It's like you've probably been told. No sleep, no life, but probably because of the sleep deprivation, you're absolutely gaga over the little shit, nonetheless."

I chuckled. "I normally wouldn't pry, but since you've been in the middle of my pitiful life, I feel like I have some leeway here. Have you and his mother made amends yet?"

The guy looked at me, and something akin to misery crossed his face.

"She was my best friend. This was all the result of a night of bad choices, and no, she won't speak to me or return my texts or calls... she's completely out of contact."

"That sucks... hell, that's almost as bad as my fucked-up life."

He chuckled humorlessly. "No, this is worse. I have a little man who'll one day demand I explain how I chased his mom off. I seriously doubt he'll be as forgiving as Martin was with your mom."

I nodded and stared down at my food. "So, it really did work out between them?"

The guy smiled at me. "Yeah, it really did. I was touched by it. My parents suck worse than most. If it wasn't for my grandpa, I would've probably ended up in foster care. To see your mom go to that much effort to make amends really touched me. I think both of them healed some that day, but watching it healed a part of me as well."

I pondered what he'd said, thinking for the first time about how it really had healed them both.

"I think what set me off was that my mom once again went behind my back on this. She caused me to lose him, then she went to talk to him without my consent."

"Would you have gone with her?" he asked.

"Hell, no, I'd have done everything in my power to keep her away from him."

The guy chuckled. "So you understand why she did it behind your back."

"Understand, yes, like, no!"

He looked at me and smiled but didn't respond.

The baby made a face and grunted, which made his dad groan. "Well, that should've been predictable. Excuse me while I go take care of this..." He took the baby's bag and the carrier with him to the restroom.

Seconds after he left, the server showed back up to refill our coffees.

"Are you his boyfriend?" she asked.

I laughed. "Hardly. Besides, how did you know he's bisexual?"

"Oh, I overheard the conversation between him and the baby's mom. You aren't that bad looking either. The two of you would make a cute couple."

I snickered. I was ready to smear his face all over his office just a few hours ago and might have done so had a certain little person not gotten in the middle of it all.

"We're on professional terms," I replied. "He worked for my mother recently."

"Oh," she replied, then winked at me. "Worked for, as in past tense?" I just stared at her as she laughed. "Well, ain't no law about dating someone who worked, as in past tense, for your mom. Just sayin'," she said as she walked away.

I hadn't really thought about what the guy looked like until now. Which is odd for me since I'm a typical gay guy in that regard and usually size up any potential men when I meet them. The man was shorter than me and definitely had a Mediterranean complexion, which usually did lots for me. I liked men with a little Latin flair.

When he came back out of the restroom, baby in hand, he sat back down to finish his food.

"Everything come out, OK?" I asked, tongue in cheek.

He groaned. "Not my favorite part of the job." He leaned over his son and tickled his belly. "We're working on potty training early, aren't we sport?" he cooed. Then in all seriousness, he said, "I've convinced myself he's going to be advanced for his age and potty train before he's a year old."

I laughed at the comment. "I'm not an expert on babies, but I'm willing to bet you'll have to wait longer than that."

He put his hand up in front of me. "Shh, I want to hear no negativity... if you will it, it'll come. At least that's what my aunt keeps telling me. So I'm willing early potty training."

I laughed again. When we finished eating, I asked him where he'd like me to take him, and he offered to get a taxi back home.

"No, I'm the reason you and Luka are out, and it looks like it could start raining any moment. I'm happy to take you home."

That's how I came to learn that Luka and his dad lived less than three blocks from my office in one of the trendiest downtown neighborhoods in Atlanta.

If I hadn't already dragged him out and almost smashed his face, I would've invited myself into the beautiful old Victorian house, just to appease my architectural curiosity. But that'd have to wait for another day. I helped him get the baby seat out of the tiny back seat and shook his hand as he took the little one inside.

As he left, I noticed the almost perfect bubble butt and wondered for the first time in my life if I wasn't a daddy chaser after all.

Trevor

Peter was different than I thought he'd be. I wasn't really that surprised when he showed up at my office angry about his mother and me snooping in his life. Hell, I'd have thrown a rib out if my mom had done that, but after he'd gotten his frustration all out, he calmed down pretty fast.

Linda was right. The man was drop-dead gorgeous. I had no pretense he'd be interested in me, though. And even if he was, I was in no position to date anyone. Luckily, my hand was still in fine working order. Not that I had the energy to even do that since I was surviving on less than two hours sleep between Luka's temper tantrums. That baby had no problem expressing his wishes or, more accurately, his demands. All those commercials where the mom is cuddling an infant who is all happy and snuggly are lies. At least they were lies when it came to Luka.

No, even if Peter was interested, I was not available. I must have sighed out loud because Aunt Doris glanced up from the crossword puzzle she was doing on the table next to my desk.

Chuckling, she teased, "Thinking about a certain someone?"

"No comment," I replied without looking at her.

"You know that man who dropped you off was quite the looker."

"Aunt Doris, that was my client's son!"

"Client's son or not, he was still a looker."

I sighed again and decided it was best to ignore my aunt. From experience, I knew she was an insatiable romantic. If the library full of romance novels, most of which were signed by the author, wasn't any indication, the fact that she tried to fix me up with every eligible bachelor she came across, straight or gay, since finding out I was bi would've been enough.

Of course, I should've known ignoring my aunt wouldn't really work either.

"So," she began, and I sighed, knowing I wasn't going to get any work done. At least not until I satisfied her curiosity. "You know I'll keep Luka if you wanted to go out on a date."

"Aunt Doris, I'm exhausted most of the time. I barely have enough energy to get my work done, I sure don't have enough *oomph* to deal with some needy lover." I turned and looked at Luka, who was sleeping in his bassinet next to me. "One needy man in my life is quite enough, thank you very much."

Aunt Doris chuckled but didn't let it go.

"You know, you'll need to get back out there sooner or later, and Luka is sleeping longer every night. He'll be on a regular sleep schedule soon enough."

"Until then, I have to keep my head down and try to get enough work done to survive."

Aunt Doris didn't respond right away, and I thought we were done with the conversation when she said, "If your parents were involved, maybe they could help out, you know, financially."

The bitterness that erupted in the form of a laugh shocked even me. "My parents have never been supportive, Aunt Doris. They gave Grandpa child support, but that was more because my dad was afraid the congregation would find out he broke my arm."

Aunt Doris sighed. "I'm sorry they aren't more supportive, Trevor. Your grandpa tried to get your mom more involved, but she's so attached to your dad she wouldn't budge for fear of offending him."

"My dad's a total ass, Aunt Doris, and mom isn't much better. I know she's your sister, but the truth is we're all better off without them in our lives. I shouldn't have even tried over Christmas. Now that they know I'm bi, I'm sure things could even get worse. I kick myself for even going over there."

Aunt Doris sat quietly again. I could feel the tension, or maybe it was sadness coming off her. I turned around and looked at her.

"You and Grandpa have always been more my parents than either of them ever was. I really don't need them in my life. Hell, it doesn't even hurt anymore. Mostly, I've figured out I just need to stay away from them and let them live their lives, and I'll live mine."

Aunt Doris put her pencil down next to the crossword book and met my expression. "I admit, I feel guilty keeping Luka from your mom, but I understand why we aren't telling her. When we were kids, we used to talk about having a family. I never really wanted to have my own kids. Even when we were young, I thought there were so many people in the world, I didn't need to add to it, but your mom seemed obsessed about having kids. When we grew up, she got married right away, and then you came along shortly after that. She was devastated when she'd learned she couldn't have any more children, so for me, I think I keep waiting for her to get her head out of her ass and figure out you are what she really wanted."

"Yeah, that isn't gonna happen as long as my dad is around. He's always hated me. Even when I was little, he'd say hateful things about how I was a nuisance. That I was just in his way. And for the record, Mom heard him and never said anything to contradict him."

Aunt Doris looked down at her lap before speaking. "I know, honey. Your grandpa and I talked about what you'd been through. We probably should've stepped in earlier, but again, we both remembered how much your mom had wanted kids. We were confused."

"It's OK," I replied as I turned back to the laptop. "Grandpa and I talked about it when I first moved in. I'd never really felt like they were my family. You and he were always my parents, and I longed for the days when one of you would come pick me up. When I finally moved in, it was like I'd won the lottery. I'm happy things worked out as they did. Now I know who they are and what they are to me." When Aunt Doris made eye contact, I said, "You don't have to worry about my mom or dad or how we are or aren't getting along. You're my family. They are distant relatives. I've got everything I need and the fact that you're helping with Luka as much as you do, well, that proves the point even more."

Aunt Doris had tears in her eyes. "You know I love you, Trevor. So did Dad." She turned toward the bassinet. "He'd have been impossible to live with had he been here when Luka came into our lives. I can't imagine how spoiled that baby would've been."

"He's pretty spoiled now."

She chuckled again, wiping at the tears. "He's perfect, and you know it."

I smiled as I looked over at Luka's sleeping form. "I'm pretty partial to him."

Aunt Doris came over and put her hand on my shoulder. She peered into the bassinet with me. "Yeah, me too."

We stayed like that for several minutes, admiring the little one. "I'm working tonight at the shop," Aunt Doris said as she turned.

"I noticed you're picking up hours again. Is there a problem?"

"Not really, we lost a couple people with the summer term break coming up, and until school starts back this fall, we probably won't be able to replace them. Just par for the course," she replied.

"Have you ever thought about selling?" I asked.

She looked at me for a moment and smiled. "Your grandpa went to work in that shop when he first moved here. He and Mom loved working there, and Rita and I used to play under the racks when we were little. It's such a part of our lives, I couldn't imagine letting it go."

Not for the first time, I wanted to encourage her to sell it and let it go. The clothing shop had been

Grandpa's dream, and he'd loved it like it was part of the family. Still, I also knew Aunt Doris hated the new clothes, and when she wasn't needed, she avoided even stepping into the place.

"I don't think Grandpa would mind if you decided to sell. Besides, you've always been more of a vintage gal than designer."

Aunt Doris laughed. "Yeah, but vintage is losing its appeal. The shop pays the bills. If I sold up, I'd have to get a real job."

We'd had this discussion off and on since I moved in at age ten. Aunt Doris volunteered all over town. At the homeless shelter, the soup kitchen, a thrift store run by her hippie friends, and various other organizations I'd lost track of. She was as hard a worker as Grandpa had ever been, but working for a living, well, that was never her strong suit.

"I don't know, Aunt Doris. The kids at school seem to be wearing vintage clothing all the time. Have you considered bringing a line of vintage into the store?"

She just laughed. "I brought it up once with your grandpa, and he almost had a heart attack. Could you imagine my funky vintage clothing next to the couture lines?"

"I guess not," I admitted. "But if you aren't going to sell, now that Grandpa is gone, and my mom isn't going to pitch in to help, you're going to have to figure out how to make that store more to your liking."

Aunt Doris just shrugged. "It'll all work out. It always does, after all."

I smiled. "There's the Aunt Doris I know and love."

She smiled too. "Don't you have work to do? All this talk of me working is giving me a headache." She stood up, kissed the top of my head like she always did when I was being dismissed, and disappeared into the kitchen.

Aunt Doris is as strong a personality as the rest of my Croatian family. I knew without a shadow of a doubt she'd figure the whole couture issue out and make it her own. Just like she did everything else in her life.

Peter

No matter what I did, I couldn't get the young father out of my head. It surprised me since I'd barely thought about another guy since Martin and I had split. That adorable sideways grin, the way he looked at his infant son, the cute bubble butt I watched while he climbed the stairs as I stood by the car watching him go into his home. All that seemed to be playing over and over in my mind.

It had been just under two months since I'd taken him home when I finally figured out an excuse to see him again. My boss pulled me into a meeting with Leonardo Richmond, a forty-year-old steampunk model turned entrepreneur. He was expanding his Neo-Victorian line of gadgets and clothing to the East Coast. Richmond saw my classical architectural designs and wanted to hire us. He thought I could modernize the Victorian architecture he was working toward into the steampunk renaissance he was hoping to achieve.

I immediately thought of the houses in Inman Park and the Gothic design of Trevor's home in particular. I quickly pulled up a picture I'd taken right after taking Trevor home and showed it to Richmond.

"My thought was to veer away from commercial property and create a first-floor level that mimicked a Gothic home similar to this one. Is that what you had in mind?" I asked.

When he saw the picture, his eyes lit up. "I knew you were the man for the job. But it can't be just the old Victorian design, the architecture has to pull the public in by saying it's both modern and Victorian at the same time."

"Not unlike your clothing line?" I asked.

"That's right, both sexy and historic."

I smiled, knowing exactly how I'd pull this off. "I happen to know the owner. If they allow it, I'd like to have you tour the property with me, and you could share with me the elements of the design you like and the ones you want me to dispose of."

The man's face beamed, and when I looked at my boss, he was smiling too. Silently, I thought there was nothing so great as catching two birds with one net. Not only did I impress my new client, but I also had the perfect excuse to visit Trevor again. And if I were really lucky, I'd talk him into going out with me.

After the meeting, I immediately walked the short distance to Trevor's home and knocked on his door.

A moment passed before a woman who appeared to be in her mid-to-late thirties opened the door and smiled at me.

"Hello, ma'am," I said. "My name is Peter Reed, and I'm an acquaintance of Trevor Kovachich."

The woman invited me in, then took my hand. "I'm Doris Kovachich, Trevor's aunt."

"Nice to meet you. Is Trevor here by chance?" I asked.

"No, I'm afraid not," she replied. "His son had a doctor's appointment this afternoon. But he should be back around five. Would you like to come back then?"

There was something in the way the woman was smiling at me that made me suspicious. Having grown up with a meddling mother and aunts, I'd become hypersensitive to family who were up to something just by seeing their expressions. Had I not had an agenda, I probably would've skipped out on the invitation and waited to come back when I knew he'd be home.

A vision of one of Richmond's steampunk contraptions quickly flashed through my mind. I immediately thought that if I was going to talk them into letting me tour the home with my new client, I'd have to grease all the parts of the machine.

So I smiled as brightly as I could. "Well, yes, ma'am, I'd like that. Can I bring something with me and treat the two of you to dinner? I'm guessing the little one keeps your hands full."

The woman grinned, and there was no missing the glint in her eye. "That would be lovely, Peter. Why don't we say six o'clock then?"

"Perfect," I replied. "How's pizza? There's a nice place around the corner."

"That'd be perfect, we both like meat lover's."

I smiled at her. "It's a date then. I'll see you both at six o'clock."

As I left, I felt a little off-kilter as I'd never invited myself over to a potential date's home for pizza before. And the ulterior motives in his aunt's face were nothing if not unsettling. However, those who played strictly by the rules never won, so even though it was all a little strange, I decided to go with it.

When I arrived with pizza in hand, both Trevor and his aunt looked just a little harried. Luka, the baby, was wailing his lungs out. When Doris came to the door, she apologized, saying they might need to take a raincheck.

"Can I take a turn holding him? Sometimes a different pair of hands can make a difference."

I had no idea if that was true or not. Still, I didn't want to lose the opportunity to meet with them about touring the house, and even if I was only able to keep the baby entertained for a moment while they got some rest and had a bite to eat, then it was worth it.

The feral glint I'd seen earlier was gone, and I only saw gratitude in her face. "It certainly couldn't hurt any," she replied.

When I walked in, Trevor was in the parlor, walking in circles with the crying baby. He turned, and I could tell he was surprised when he saw me. "Peter came by earlier, and I invited him to dinner. I forgot to tell you since Luka was so upset," his aunt said.

Trevor attempted a smile, but I could tell the crying was getting the better of him. "Here, give me a moment with the baby," I offered. "Sometimes, babies like me."

Trevor hesitated for a moment. But when he turned toward his aunt, she nodded, and he relented. Doris took the pizza from me, and Trevor slipped the baby into my arms.

My arms were warm from carrying the pizza, which is probably why the little one calmed as quickly as he did. He began quieting down almost immediately.

The other adults both stared at me with wonder, like I'd performed a miracle, and I certainly wasn't above taking credit for his calming down.

It's just natural, I guess, that when a baby is put in your arms, you turn into a human rocking chair. I gently bounced the little one in my arms as I told his dad and great aunt to go have pizza while I kept the little one busy. They both agreed, and the look of wonder never left their faces.

I followed them into the kitchen behind the parlor. I immediately appreciated the renovation that had converted what was probably a library at one point into a large kitchen that spanned the back of the house. It wrapped around the back of the large staircase that was the first thing I'd seen when entering through the front door.

Both of them tore into the food while I admired for the first time how cute this little one really was. I'm not what you'd call a baby person, despite the fact that I'd been stuck with baby cousins all my life. My mom was quite a bit older than my aunts, so I was born first, and the two years between me and my first cousins had made me the perfect babysitter.

As the little one fell asleep in my arms, I walked around humming to him, hoping this would last long enough for me to ask for the tour. And maybe if I was lucky, a drink with his weary-looking father.

By the time Trevor and his aunt had finished eating, Luka was fast asleep, and Trevor stood to take him from me. His aunt stopped him, though. "You know, there's a ninety percent chance if you pick him up, he'll start screaming again."

Trevor's hands immediately went up into the air. "Good point," he said. "Sorry, Peter, I'm afraid you've got yourself baby duty. I don't think either of us could take another screaming fit for a while."

I laughed quietly. "No problem. Any idea why he was so upset?"

"Oh yeah, he had his first set of immunizations, and he was none too happy about it."

"The boy has a way of making his feelings known," Doris added.

"I see that," I chuckled.

"So I'm assuming you didn't come over here just to babysit my bundle of very loud joy. How can we help you?"

I cocked an eyebrow at the *we* part, amused at how he'd included his aunt in the conversation.

"I have an odd request," I began. "I'm an architect with Littman and Rowe, and we recently signed a new client who is big into steampunk art. Your home is exactly what he wants to recreate for his stores. I was wondering if you'd let me bring him over for a tour to get an idea of how he'd like to set the project up."

Doris's eyes lit up. "Oh, I love steampunk! Who's your client?"

I hesitated. Unfortunately, I'd forgotten to get Richmond's permission to share that information with them, so I had to shrug. "I'm sorry, I need to get his permission before I tell you. However, if you're interested, I'll ask my client if he minds."

"I'm very interested," she said. "I just *love* steampunk. All that sexy merged with the old Victorian styles."

I could tell I'd hit the jackpot with the aunt. I turned to her nephew to get his perspective. Unfortunately, what I saw in his face was much more guarded.

"You know, Peter, we have a very vocal little one, and he isn't very keen on traveling. It might be a bad time to bring people over."

"I'll tell you what, my firm has a daycare program for employees. If I can get them to agree to care for Luka while we're touring the home, would you be OK with it then?"

Trevor wasn't convinced by my suggestion. I saw a clear look of protective dad cross his face. I almost chuckled but knew it probably wouldn't go over well.

"If it helps, the daycare won several awards last summer for superior care, and the firm has gotten awards for being innovative enough to have a daycare in the building."

Trevor still wasn't convinced but agreed to talk it over with his aunt and get back to me.

After that discussion, we chatted about easier things. Trevor wanted to know how my mom was doing, and I let him know we were on better terms now that she'd cleared things up with Martin.

I'd been surprised at how much better I'd felt after Trevor and I had met that day. He'd helped me see that my mom had done what she did out of love for me and sincerely regretted her part in my breakup with Martin. It's like a part of my emotions were dammed up. Once mom had resolved things with Martin, the gates had opened, and the floodwaters had receded.

He smiled when I told him. He had a genuine affinity for my mom, which caused me to want to get to know him even more. I'd always figured if I ever dated again, my mom would be off-limits after what she'd done to Martin.

I wasn't ready to propose or anything. Still, the thought that I could possibly have a relationship, even date someone who could or would tolerate the infamous Matilda Reed, was a definite plus.

Trevor

I didn't trust Peter Reed. There ya go. I said it. The whole bringing pizza over to the house was suspicious. And his proposal for me leaving my baby with strangers, well, that was a big old ugly red flag. I'd be damned if I did such a thing. No, if Peter really wanted to tour our house, then he'd do it with Luka right where he belongs!

Oh, not to mention the whole, "I have to get permission before I can reveal his name." Well, buddy, you'll be revealing his name, and I'll be doing a thorough background check before anyone comes into my house. That much I can promise you!

My aunt might be gullible, but I'm not. The one good thing about being the kid of a monster, you learn quickly how to see everyone you meet as a potential threat. The way "too good-looking for his own good" Peter Reed was definitely a potential threat.

If it hadn't been for meeting his mom first, I'd have thrown his suspicious ass to the curb the minute he walked into my home. Oh, and let's not forget how quickly Luka warmed up to him. That was suspicious too. After Peter left, I admit I searched for needle marks. Somehow that man had drugged my baby. It took everything in me not to take him back to the doctor to have him examined by a professional. I even mentioned something to that effect to my aunt, and she just laughed at me.

"Luka's a smart baby, Trevor. He just knows a handsome piece of man when he sees one."

"Whatever!" I exclaimed when I changed Luka's diaper later that evening. I did another thorough check, but nothing appeared out of place, and Luka was back to his grumpy self anyway, so if he had been drugged, it wasn't something that lasted long.

I'd done a background check on Peter when his mom had first hired me, so I pretty much knew his backstory. He'd graduated with honors from the University of Texas. From there, he was hired by a large firm in Austin and immediately won some big prestigious award for his modern twist on Greek Revival.

Everything about the man was glowing. He was a golden child, which, of course, must mean he had to have some kind of weird kink, or he was a serial killer. Either way, I wasn't going to turn my back on him anytime soon.

The next day, I decided I needed to give my client, Mrs. Matilda Reed, a courtesy phone call to check-in. My investigator's instincts that I'd acquired in the months I'd worked there were kicking in, and I assumed I could get a better picture of what her son was up to after we talked.

"Oh, what a pleasure!" the woman exclaimed when I told her who it was.

I genuinely smiled. Mrs. Reed had hit a soft spot inside me, and it felt good to speak to her again. Almost forgetting my agenda, I asked, "So how are you and Martin?"

"Oh, so much better. Do you know he even sent me a thank you card? I've already responded with a letter thanking him. I can't thank you enough, Trevor, it's like a ton of bricks have been lifted from my shoulders," she said.

For the life of me, I couldn't imagine Mrs. Reed being anything but the gracious Southern belle she appeared to be. But I'd heard enough to know she'd done a nasty job on Martin, and I quickly realized that whoever Peter fell in love with should be incredibly careful around this one.

I had no doubt, though, the successful Peter Reed would land some famous model or fancy businessman. He didn't look the type to slum it with just anyone. Even Martin was easy on the eyes. Dark features accented with long eyelashes and dramatically blue eyes made him appear powerfully masculine with just the right touches of femininity. The combination would make any warm-blooded gay or bi man want to pull him into an embrace and never let go.

"So, how are things with Peter now?" I was trying to learn more about Peter without giving away my investigation. Unfortunately, she thought I wanted to know how their relationship was.

"You were right on that front as well. Peter and I are talking again." I heard the tears in her voice. "It's such a relief having him back in my life. I will never be able to repay you for that."

I decided to take another tack and mentioned that he'd come by the office.

"I'm so happy it's worked out, Mrs. Reed. You know I met him, Peter, that is. He came by the office the Monday after we got back from Florida."

She grew quiet before asking how that went.

"Trevor, I'm so sorry about that. Did it go OK?" I could hear the concern in her voice.

I chuckled. "Better than you'd have thought. He was angry when I first met him, but Luka, my son, won him over quickly enough."

That sent her on a tangent, where she mentioned Peter's strange ability with babies and dogs. "Since he was a little boy, no matter how aggressive a dog was or how angry a baby was, they seemed to calm right away when he was around."

My suspicious mind immediately thought they must be in it together, so I came out and asked directly. "So did Peter mention that he'd come to see me?"

Matilda laughed out loud. "No, Peter wouldn't have told me. I'm not surprised he came to you, though. I purposefully didn't tell him who you were, but I guess he figured it out some other way."

"Yeah, he told me Martin gave him my name."

"My Peter could've been an investigator himself," she replied. "He's always been good at getting to the bottom of things."

I smiled. You could hear the love for her son in her voice. Again, the pang of hearing a mom talk about her son in such a proud way resonated with me, and I felt sad that my mom couldn't have given a crap whether I lived or died.

"Mrs. Reed, I have to go, but I'm glad everything worked out. If you need anything else, please let me know, OK?" I asked before ending the phone call.

"You know," she said before she let me hang up, "you and Peter have a lot in common. You should really spend some time together. I worry that he doesn't have enough *friends* in Atlanta." The word "friends" was said in that way moms do when they mean anything but.

"Thanks, Mrs. Reed, but with the baby and work, I'm afraid I wouldn't make a particularly good friend for anyone at the moment. You have a great day, and again, let me know if you need anything else."

I hung up before she had time to push the issue again.

By some strange coincidence, Peter called moments after I hung up with his mother. Something was really off about all this. Now I was plotting all kinds of conspiracy theories in my head. Mrs. Reed, Peter, and Martin setting up some kind of theft sting or something, except we didn't really have the kind of money that would be worth trying to steal. The mortgage on the house was pretty low, but we still had one, and since Grandpa died, the shop's bottom line was awfully close to the red. If they were trying to rob us, they were definitely barking up the wrong tree.

I answered the phone but wasn't overly friendly. "Rainelle's Investigation, Trevor speaking." I decided to keep things professional even though I knew it was Peter.

"Hi, Trevor, it's Peter Reed," he continued in the same professional manner. "I got permission to share with you my client's name and wondered if we could set up a date for him to tour your home."

I waited for him to give me the name before responding.

Peter seemed to stumble over my lack of questioning, and having him off-center was exactly where I wanted him.

"His name is Leonardo Richmond. He's an entrepreneur with shops in London and Paris. Have you heard of him?"

I admitted that I hadn't. I didn't add that, soon enough, I'd know everything I could about him.

"So, Mr. Richmond is currently in New York, but he'll be coming back to town on the fifteenth for a few days. Would it be OK to set up a time to tour your home then?"

I waited a moment while I pretended to thumb through a calendar that didn't exist on my desk. "Peter, I can't answer that right now. Can I call you back?"

I could hear the smile in Peter's voice. "That would be fine. Thanks, Trevor."

I was just about to hang up when Peter asked, "Until then"—I hesitated, waiting to hear what else he had in mind—"would you consider meeting me for a drink?"

I had always been good at picking up on emotions, and I could hear the nervousness in Peter's question. My suspicious mind immediately told me even if he were a crook, he'd likely have nerves while setting his plans in motion.

"I'm sorry Peter, with the baby and work, I just don't have time."

Peter genuinely sounded disappointed when he replied, "Oh." Then he chimed back in. "I talked to my company, and they said as long as you can prove Luka's had all immunizations that are required by the state, then they could take Luka when we bring Mr. Richmond over."

"We'll see, Peter," I said, not giving him any misconception that I was interested. "I'll talk to Aunt Doris about the fifteenth, and one of us will get back to you. Thanks, Peter. Bye."

I hung up before he could respond. I wanted to do a lot more research before I committed to anything.

Peter was a beautiful man, and I admit he caused my spine to tingle when I looked at him, but I had too many precious things to protect. Tingling spines had to take a back seat to my family.

Peter

Trevor's walls were definitely up, but I wasn't really that surprised. I'm guessing I'd be the same way if I had an infant to protect. I'd have to move a little slower if I was going to get anywhere with him.

His aunt Doris called me the next day and was all but yelling with excitement. I guess she knew of Richmond and his steampunk designs. She helped me set a date to tour her and Trevor's home. I didn't ask about Trevor as I assumed since she'd called, he was having cold feet.

I did ask about whether Trevor needed a babysitter, and Doris went quiet. "No, I don't think that'll be necessary," she said. Just the way she said it made it clear he wasn't as interested in this as she was. Oh well, at least I'd get to show the home to Richmond, and then I could start putting together the designs I'd already started forming in my mind.

I pulled my computer out and sculpted the image of the Kovachich house from memory. I especially loved the big tower that rose from the top. I had ideas to add a clock with steampunk gears as an accent instead of the windows that accented the towers of the home.

The interior of the Kovachich home retained all the delicious dark mahogany and walnut, which I'd also wanted to incorporate in the interior of the store. I was hoping if we got this planned correctly that we'd be able to incorporate the basic design features into every store, giving consistency to Richmond's brand.

It was the interior I wanted him to see, as that was really the most important element of the design. In my mind, the stores needed just enough Victorian features to entice people to buy, but not so much that it discouraged the more modern buyer.

Considering that most of Richmond's customers were Millennials, it made that a very tight rope to walk.

I didn't mind the baby being at the showing. In fact, I kinda like the idea that Trevor was so protective. I remember when he first learned about being a dad and the overwhelmed expression on his face as he left the diner. Knowing he'd settled into parenthood made me feel hopeful for little Luka.

Doris agreed to let me come over and take pictures of their home, but Trevor was conveniently not available when I did. That hurt my ego a bit. I'd hoped to see him and even the little one, but I shouldn't be too disappointed when the house was so perfect and convenient for the job.

I sent the pictures to Richmond, and he responded almost immediately. He was surprised how close the home was to what he was dreaming about. "You're like some kind of mind reader," he replied.

"Make sure you tell my boss that, will you?" I emailed back.

When the fifteenth arrived, I took Richmond to the house. Trevor was present along with little Luka. On the one hand, we were lucky the little one was content during our visit, but on the other, I sort of wished I could hold him again as well as spend copious amounts of time staring at his dad. However, knowing

I needed to spend time with my client quashed that fantasy.

Richmond and Doris hit it off immediately, and she told him about how she'd designed a few clothes after seeing him walk the runway in Paris. She told us her dad owned the couture and designer clothing shop downtown and that she went to school to be a clothing designer but never liked what her dad sold, so she'd given it up.

The way my client was flirting with Doris, I barely got a word in edgewise. While the two of them flirted, I took more pictures and jotted down ideas that I could discuss with him when we got back to the office.

When Doris took Richmond upstairs, I decided to stay in the parlor with Trevor and the baby. I said something to the effect that I was going to stay down there, but neither my client nor Doris seemed to have heard me.

I sat down across from Trevor and laughed. "I think I've ceased to be of any importance."

Trevor smiled back at me. "Yeah, the two of them fit like gears in a well-tuned clock."

"Touché," I replied. "Any chance I'll get my client back by the end of the day?"

"Truth is, I've never seen Aunt Doris so starstruck. I remember when she went through her steampunk stage. Hell, I think she still has an attic full of her designs. I'm guessing she's gonna drag him up there to see it all."

I sighed. "I admit, I was hoping to get started on his designs tomorrow. I have another client I'm supposed to start with next month, so I sort of needed to have these designs at least well on their way to being done."

"You know how strongly opinionated your mom is?" he asked.

I nodded. "Well, magnify that by fifty percent, and that's Aunt Doris. Once she gets her mind set on something, she doesn't let it go easily."

Peter sighed. "I'm guessing before she's done, she'll have an opinion or two about my designs."

Trevor laughed quietly, trying not to upset Luka. "Sorry about that, I could've warned you before you asked to tour the house."

"Yeah, thanks for that late piece of information."

"If it helps, she's incredibly brilliant."

I smiled. "Yeah, I can tell. Your home is so beautiful."

Trevor looked around. "That was mostly my grandmother, I think... I didn't really know her. Unfortunately, she died when I was a baby."

Things got awkward then as we sat across from one another, unsure what to talk about next. Luka stirred, and Trevor began to bounce him in his arms.

"Can I hold him for a minute?" I asked.

"It's a risk, you know he could start wailing at any moment, and he doesn't do well with transfers."

"I'll take the risk, if you trust me."

Trevor looked at me with narrowed eyes for a moment. I thought to myself, *no, he doesn't trust me even a little bit,* but he handed the baby over, nonetheless.

I really liked this little guy and it felt good just to sit in the antique rocker in the beautiful old parlor and rock him.

Trevor had an odd expression on his face, then he turned away. "If you've got him, I'm going to use the bathroom. I've been holding it since shortly after y'all got here. I was just afraid if I moved, he'd blow a gasket."

I couldn't help but laugh. "Go on, we'll be fine."

Luka woke up while I was holding him and looked up at me with those blue eyes, which stirred something deep inside me. It amazed me how babies held such power over people. I barely knew this little one, and I already felt a need to protect him. I guess that was God's way of helping babies who were so helpless to survive in a such cruel and vicious world.

Trevor

When I came back, Peter and Luka were staring at each other, and Peter was singing some lullaby to him.

I'd not heard those lyrics before, but the tune sounded slightly familiar.

The sight did strange things to my insides that I couldn't quite explain. Not to mention Peter had an amazing voice.

I stayed in the hall watching the two for a moment longer. "Your mom told me you have some kind of magic touch with dogs and babies. I think she may be right."

Peter glanced up from the baby and winked, but didn't stop singing. When he finished the verse, he said, "My mom is a little biased when it comes to me. I wouldn't put much weight in her beliefs regarding my magical abilities."

I chuckled. "She does adore you, I caught onto that pretty quickly after we met."

Peter smiled as he looked back down at Luka.

"Maybe I need to hire you to babysit from time to time."

"I don't know if you can afford me. Last I checked my mom paid my babysitter fifteen dollars per night, which, of course, I thought was highway robbery."

I laughed. "I might be able to afford that. How did you know how much your mom paid your babysitter?"

"I asked her, of course. She was my teenage neighbor, and I was more than pissed that my mother had hired someone to watch me. At nine years old, I was convinced if my friend Paul could be a latch key kid, I was more than old enough to take care of myself while my mom went out. I remember confronting my neighbor about taking advantage of my mom. She wasn't very amused."

I chuckled. "I'm guessing that goes with parenting, and I remember being nine and thinking I was grown up."

We chatted about childhood until Aunt Doris and Mr. Richmond came back down the stairs, both laughing and talking a mile a minute.

"Mr. Richmond said he'd like to use our home for his kickoff party since it's the inspiration for his store's design. What do you think, Trevor?" she asked with the look of a star-struck teenager.

"That sounds fun... when do you think this party will happen?"

We all turned toward Peter, who shrugged. "I'm not sure. The designs will take several months to finish and get Mr. Richmond's approval. Then the building can take up to a couple years depending on how complex it is. To be safe, I'd plan for two years."

My aunt appeared crestfallen. Mr. Richmond noticed. "Why don't we do an introductory party to build some excitement for the store? I could even hire a few models to demonstrate what the clothing line will look like."

Aunt Doris's face changed until she was beaming. "That sounds great!" she replied. "We can have the house ready for a fall party, and that gives us plenty of time to get the parking permits pulled for the event. How many people do you think will show up?"

"It could be hundreds," Mr. Richmond estimated. "I'll keep it pretty narrow in scope though, maybe just focus on Atlanta's VIPs along with the press. Exclusive tends to make things more appealing for the press anyway."

I thought my aunt might end up bursting at any moment with excitement.

"Sounds like a fun plan, Mr. Richmond. Does my aunt have your number just in case she has questions?"

When she turned toward me, I winked at her subtly. She sent me a nasty look, but I ignored her as Mr. Richmond gave her his phone number.

"This is my mobile number when I'm in the States, but here's my card with my European number, as well as my email address. If you send me an email, we can make plans between now and then."

I glanced at Peter, and both of us just about laughed out loud at how obvious the two of them were being. Peter stood up and handed Luka back to me. "I bet the two of them will have a date planned by tomorrow," he whispered as he put Luka in my arms.

"More like by tonight," I whispered back.

Aunt Doris escorted Peter and Mr. Richmond out into the entryway. Peter said goodbye and walked out while Mr. Richmond lingered in the doorway a little longer. I couldn't hear what he and Aunt Doris were saying, but I could guess.

When she came back into the parlor, she had a blush on her cheeks.

"So when's the date?" I asked.

"Why do you think I have a date?" she asked with some venom.

"Oh, sorry, did I misinterpret how you two were looking at one another?"

She huffed, but when she landed in the chair across from me, a smile crossed her face. "For your information, it isn't a date. We're going to meet tonight at the restaurant next to his hotel to make preliminary plans for the party."

I quickly glanced down at Luka to keep my smile from being too obvious, but she caught it anyway.

"You think you're clever, don't you? Well, I noticed you and young Peter Reed seemed to be getting along pretty well. So, there's that!" she said with mirth in her voice.

"I don't have a date, though."

"Because you won't give him a chance," she said. "He's mighty cute, Trevor. Mighty cute."

"Again," I said, while lifting Luka slightly, "I remind you my hands are a little full at the moment."

"Pish posh," she said, surprising me with the old expression my grandpa used to use. "We both know you're using Luka as an excuse. Go out with him, if for no other reason than just to have a night out to let your hair down. You'll be a better parent if you let yourself have a little personal time, Trevor. Luka doesn't need you one hundred percent of the time, and you totally need to do something for yourself."

I sighed and stared out the window. "I'd feel guilty the entire time I was out."

"Well, you shouldn't feel guilty about me. I love looking after Luka, at least when he isn't screaming his lungs out."

We both laughed before Aunt Doris continued, "Promise me if he invites you out that you won't say no, even if it's just for lunch."

I didn't tell her he'd already invited me out for a drink. Instead, I just nodded. "If he invites me, I'll consider it."

"That's all I can ask." She jumped up and kissed the top of my head, then kissed Luka. "I'm going to go see if any of my steampunk outfits still fit. I think this meeting calls for one of my old designs. Ooh, I'm so excited." She all but skipped to the stairs, then danced up them.

I kissed Luka's head. "I think your great aunt Doris is a little star-struck."

Luka gave me an expression that looked a whole lot like, "Well, duh!"

Peter

It took everything in me not to laugh as I drove Richmond back to my office. He was like a teenage boy who'd just developed his first crush. Doris was a beautiful woman, and she'd definitely inherited the same dark complexion and bright blue eyes that stirred me when I looked at her nephew.

"I'd think a model like yourself would've been dripping with women," I said off the cuff.

Richmond turned toward me with wide eyes. "Not all women are created the same," he replied. "The beautiful Doris is special, *unique en son genre.*"

"One of a kind," I translated, and the older man patted my shoulder like I was a child. "I'm thinking her nephew is *unique en son genre* as well," I replied.

"Ooh, you like the boy, huh?"

I nodded. "Yeah, very much, but he won't give me much time."

"Does he like men as well? He has a baby, no?"

"He does, but he's bisexual. I overheard him when Luka's mom gave the baby to him."

Richmond looked at me strangely. "You would be willing to date a man with a newborn baby but no mama to care for him?"

I thought for a moment. "I guess. I haven't really thought about it. I just like Trevor."

"Parenting was never for me," he said. "Babies require too much time and energy. I've always enjoyed being selfish too much, and if I became a papa, I'd have to give more to the baby than to myself."

"That's true," I agreed. "I never thought having a child of my own was possible since I'm gay, so I never really thought about it. But I'm not opposed to it, something about being able to give so much of yourself to someone you love. It sounds fairly poetic to me."

Richmond smiled at me. "Any father who has a newborn baby he is caring for by himself would be a fool not to grab onto you and not let go. Besides, you are a very handsome man. If I liked men, I'd try to date you."

I couldn't help but laugh out loud at that. "I'll take that as a compliment. Maybe you can convince his aunt to help fix me up with him. I'm not doing a very good job on my own."

"It's a deal. I'll talk to her tonight about it."

"Tonight?" I asked. "You already have a date with Doris tonight?"

"Well, of course!" Richmond exclaimed. "I'm French, or mostly French. My grandpapa would disown me if I let such a beautiful woman get away from me."

I laughed again. "Trevor was right. I said you'd have a date with her by tomorrow, and he said it would be more like tonight."

Richmond gave me a surprised but amused smirk. "You and your *amour* bet on when we'd have a date?"

"Yep, and I lost."

Richmond laughed that rich, deep laugh that I'm sure caused many women, and men for that matter, to swoon. "I think I like you more now, Peter, than I did before. You are a romantic like me."

I smiled at the thought but was immediately hit with a pang when I remembered I hadn't been that much of a romantic, considering I let one love go without a fight. I resolved then that if I was ever lucky enough to love another man, I'd never let him slip through my fingers, no matter what.

Trevor

Luka and I came downstairs the next morning to find my aunt dancing around the kitchen. At first, she didn't notice us, so I just leaned against the door frame and watched her. Luka finally gave us away when he gurgled, then burped.

When Aunt Doris saw us, she danced over and hugged us both.

"I take it the date went well," I said.

"Oh, it went really well," she said as she twirled back over to the eggs and bacon she was frying on the stove.

I chuckled and took Luka into the parlor for our morning rocking. We'd come up with a routine that worked well for us. He usually didn't wake up in the morning until I was finished with my shower.

Then I'd feed him his first bottle, and after he finished it, I'd wander downstairs while I burped him.

Something about the jarring of the stairs seemed to be the best way to burp him anyway.

Aunt Doris would usually fix breakfast unless she was headed off to do something she'd volunteered for or if she had to work at the shop. Then I would hand Luka over to her for her morning dose of loving. Luka loved mornings and seldom threw his profound fits, instead, saving those for later in the day. God help any of us if we tried to take him out of his comfort zone in the afternoon or early evening.

"So, tell me all about it," I said as Aunt Doris handed me a plate and took Luka from me.

"Oh, the date wasn't all that special. We met at his hotel's restaurant, but we have so much in common! We ended up talking until late in the evening. Did you know his mom is French and his dad is British? I think I probably read that somewhere, but I'd forgotten until he told me. Anyway, his dad died when he was little, so he and his mom went to live with his grandpa in Paris."

"That explains the French accent," I replied, only half interested in hearing about my aunt's new boo.

"Oh, isn't it the sexiest accent? I love the French. They just have the most romantic personalities." She glanced over at me and smiled. "He kissed my hand several times. But oh my heart, before I came home, he pulled me into an embrace and kissed me like no man ever has."

She sighed and nuzzled Luka.

I finished my breakfast while she talked and stood to wash off my plate and put it in the dishwasher. "Thanks for breakfast," I said. "And I'm so happy you and Mr. Richmond got along so well. Are you going to see him again?"

My aunt smiled a mischievous smile. "Why yes, and I need to talk to you about that. Leo needs to meet with Peter tonight about the designs, so I invited them both over for dinner. I thought that way, we wouldn't have to get a sitter, and we could both spend time with two sexy men."

I gave my aunt a suspicious look, and she had the good grace to blush. "You're playing set-up, aren't you?"

She pulled a blank look of innocence. "Honey, I have no idea what you mean."

That was all the evidence I needed. We may have originated from Croatia, but my aunt had embraced the Southern belle persona with gusto. Instead of steampunk, I'm surprised she didn't have a wardrobe full of hoop skirts.

"Just remember, I only promised to consider going out with him. I never promised anything more," I said.

"Hey, can you watch Luka for a bit? If we are going to have Peter and Leonardo over for dinner, I think I'm going to make Grandpa's scampi alla busara. You know he'll haunt us if we don't serve his signature dish."

"I've got the baby, but Leo said he's bringing over wine and dessert, so no need to buy those."

"Perfect, I'll just make the shrimp then and pick up some nice bread if the French bakery around the corner isn't already sold out. We should probably serve soup, too, but I don't want to cook all day to make Grandpa's cream soup. I'll see what they have at the grocery today."

"Sounds great! We'll be here cuddling, won't we, little Luka?" I heard her crooning to him as I darted out the door.

As I turned the key in Grandpa's old car, I sighed with relief when the engine hit... the poor old thing wasn't long for this world, I thought just how lucky I was that Aunt Doris was there for me. I couldn't imagine having to pack Luka up just to make a quick run to the grocery store. As I drove, I thought about Lisa again and how difficult it was for single moms like her to survive. Part of me would always resent her for leaving Luka and not at least trying to be part of his life, but another part of me understood.

I went into our little neighborhood store and was greeted by a number of Grandpa's older friends and acquaintances. When they heard I was making his scampi recipe, the lady behind the counter darted out back and within minutes had everything I needed. I guess fifty years of making the same dish and buying the ingredients in the same store had its perks.

I received a wary eye, however, when I told them I needed some sort of soup to serve with the meal, but they didn't give me much grief as they packaged up their potato soup. I knew my grandpa would be disappointed, but seriously, I was raising a baby, and

I had a shit ton of work to get done before Peter and Leonardo showed up for dinner.

I was lucky because the little bakery around the corner still had several loaves of French bread left. It was the best bakery in town, and since opening a couple years before, they tended to sell out of everything before ten. The scampi used bread instead of noodles, so I needed good bread. Grocery store bread just wasn't going to cut it.

I'd finished the shopping so quickly, I thought I should take advantage of the time and run over to the park. I packed the shrimp into the refrigerated bag we kept in the car and drove over to Springvale Park. I'd fallen in love with the park when I was a boy, and my grandpa and aunt would take me there to hang out or play on the playground.

I got out and walked directly to the lake and sat on the same bench I'd sat on with Grandpa last time I was here. Luckily no one was out and about yet except a few kids on the playground, so I had enough space to have the talk I really wanted to have.

"Grandpa," I said quietly, hoping no one could hear me, "I need some guidance. As you probably know, I now have a baby of my own, and although Aunt Doris is helping out, I worry that I'm not going to be enough. That I don't have what it takes to be a good dad. I keep having the same nightmare over and over that I somehow broke his arm. Like dad did to me."

It was the first time I'd admitted that out loud, and the emotions around that dream crept up on me with a vengeance. Before I could stop myself, I was crying, and I was not shedding delicate tears. No, I was crying like a crazy person.

Before I knew it, a hand rested on my shoulder. My first thought was Grandpa. But when I looked up and saw Peter's face, I was full-out mortified.

"Fuck," I said out loud, quickly wiping at my tears. "I thought I was alone."

"You were. Sorry, I drive through the park to get to work. When I saw you get out of your car, I followed you."

"Well, shit. Now you think I'm insane?"

"No, I don't. I know you have to be under intense pressure raising Luka on your own." Peter sat next to me, then put his arm around me and pulled me to his chest. Damn, if that wasn't the worst thing he could've done. I came here to have a pity fest, and I sure didn't need anyone to witness it. But the stress of raising Luka, learning to be a dad, and now, fuck, Peter... Peter was part of the stress. Thinking about dating again was what pushed me over the edge.

Instead of pulling away from Peter, like any sane person would, I let him hold me while my tears flowed. Luckily, I wasn't one to linger on my emotions for long, and so after I got my cryfest done and over with, I pulled back. "I'm so sorry, Peter. You caught me at a really bad time. I should be getting back."

"Wait, I'm the one who should be sorry for getting in the way of a moment to yourself, but when I saw you were upset, I couldn't help it. It seemed like you might need someone by your side."

I wiped the tears, then let my head fall back on the bench. "Peter, I'm in no shape to be dating anyone right now. When my aunt told me you and Leonardo were coming for dinner tonight, I sort of flipped. On the one hand, I rushed to the store to buy ingredients for dinner, and on the other, I'm an emotional train wreck."

I looked around at the lake and the trail that worked its way around it. "This is the last place I sat with my grandpa before he died. He's the one I could talk to about anything. Sex, friendships, I even had a long conversation with him once about whether or not I should use drugs when a friend in middle school was trying to get me to try them. When Luka's mom left him with me, I was shocked and scared shitless, but I knew as long as I had Aunt Doris, I'd be fine... we'd be fine. When I went on that trip with your mom, I didn't worry about him one bit, knowing my aunt would keep him safe. Now, she's met someone and is so giddy over him. I've never seen her that way, and all I can think about is she's going to end up moving to Europe, and what the hell am I going to do then? I know, I know, it's selfish and cruel of me to wish Leonardo never showed up, but the fear is there, nonetheless. Then this morning, she told me you were going to come over, and I could tell this was a set-up and, Peter, even if you are interested in me, which you probably aren't, but even if you were, I can't date someone. I have a baby. I just graduated from college, and I couldn't even find the time to walk across the damned stage. There's no way I can date someone, be a new parent, and continue to function like a normal human being."

Peter listened to me rant, and even though the embarrassment grew as the words spewed from my mouth, I wasn't capable of stopping them.

Finally, Peter leaned back, keeping his arm around me. "If you're so worried about dating, then let's not date. Let's just hang out together. No strings, no commitments, just two guys hanging out." He stared at me with a look of concern on his face. "I'm sorry I put pressure on you. I didn't mean to, but I do like you, I liked you from the minute I met you even if I did want to tar and feather you for interfering with my life. But in the short time I've known you, everything has turned into something good. First, you got my mother to apologize to Martin, and Martin actually forgave her. I don't even have words for how important that was or how that healed all three of us. Then your home was exactly what my client needed, and we're building his shops around its architecture. And you, I don't want to put any more pressure on you but, to be honest, you are the first guy I've met since Martin left that I want to get to know better. That means something to me. I wondered if I'd ever date again and now, I can see that it's possible. So even if you aren't interested in dating me, I want to get to know you better. I want to get to know Luka better, too. It'd be fun for me to spend some time with a baby. So, if you're willing, let's try that, OK?"

Peter's look was hopeful, almost childlike, and I smiled. "I don't understand what a handsome man like you sees in a sleep-deprived single dad, but sure, I'd like to have someone to hang out with, too. Maybe the friend thing might work."

Peter's smile grew mischievous. "Can I be a friend that kisses you?"

I gazed at him, then down at his very luscious lips, and before I could stop myself, I leaned into him, taking his mouth with my own. All the concern and frustration bubbled into that kiss as I pulled his head closer. My tongue tangled with his, and the heat magnified instantly. Luckily, he pulled back and sighed. "Let's do this again when you aren't feeling so vulnerable." Then he looked around and said, "If that gets any deeper, we're going to turn Springvale Park into a porn scene."

I knew I was blushing. One minute I was saying, "Let's be friends," and the next I almost humped him in the park.

"You'd be wise just to run away and never see me again," I whined.

"Um, after that kiss, you can bet that's *not* gonna happen. I'm going to be like a lost puppy now following you around, begging for another kiss like that one."

I chuckled. "You can't say you weren't warned."

Peter smiled and pulled me up with him. "I need to get to work. Richmond has my day filled from now"–he looked at his watch–"until tonight."

"I need to get back, too. I'm sure Aunt Doris is going to be ready for a break by the time I get home."

Peter kissed my forehead, peered into my eyes, and just as it appeared he was about to come in for round two, he pulled me into a hug. "I'll see you tonight," he said and turned to leave.

He turned around again and smiled that million-dollar smile at me, and it took all I had to keep my knees from melting under me. "I'm so screwed," I said out loud. Then he turned away and jogged toward the parking lot. "So fucking screwed," I said again as I shook my head.

Peter

When I saw Trevor get out of his car, I thought it must be providence and pulled in beside him and parked. I watched as he walked over to the bench, sat down, and looked around. I got out of my car and walked toward him, reaching him just in time to see him start sobbing.

My first thought was I should get back in my car and drive away, but he looked so alone sitting on that park bench, I couldn't help but reach out to him. I spent a significant amount of time thinking it must be really hard to find out one minute that you're a dad and the next minute have a week-old infant thrust into your sole care. I can't imagine that kind of pressure.

I didn't mean for him to kiss me. I was all ready to pull back completely and just be the friend I knew he needed right now. Hell, I was even going to offer to be his babysitter, when he laid the most intense, amazing kiss on me I'd had, well, maybe ever. The old saying of being kissed so hard it curled your toes is no joke. I literally felt my toes curl with that kiss.

I think part of my soul separated from my heart when I forced myself to pull away from him. It'd been so long since I kissed a man. Way too long, apparently. I didn't kiss hookups, so the last guy I kissed was my friend Joshua. Well, he wasn't my friend at the time, but that had been awkward and well, wrong. Even if his dad hadn't split us up, we'd have done it ourselves.

But kissing Trevor, that was one of the best things I think I've ever done. It took every ounce of my willpower to kiss his forehead and leave. All I wanted to do was kiss that amazing mouth again. Well, of course, my mind thought of a lot of other thoughts at the same time, but if I was going to work on being this man's friend first, it wouldn't do to think about all the other stuff I wanted to do to him... or have him do to me.

Shit, Peter, I thought to myself, *that man is someone's dad for God's sake. Are you really thinking about him in a pornographic way?* Yes. I'm definitely thinking of him in a pornographic way... oh, the things I could do to that bubble butt...

OK, this has to stop, or Leonardo Richmond wasn't going to see me anytime soon since I was going to have to go back to my condo and stand for an hour under an ice-cold shower.

I made myself think of the architectural designs I wanted to chat with Richmond about. Amazing, I never thought of architectural designs as sexy before, but after that kiss, even walls and floors seemed sexy as hell to me. A certain gothic home was exceptionally sexy.

I arrived at the office, got out of the car, readjusted to make sure I didn't have a full tent in the front of my pants, looked down, sighed, and moved my briefcase to hide my discomfort.

Luckily, when I walked into the office, the chaos that seemed to be a daily part of my firm's life was in full swing. Nothing was a better mood killer than suits running around like a bunch of feral cats who'd just been freed from their cages.

I saw Richmond and my boss sitting in the conference room, and headed that way.

When Richmond saw me, he smiled and stood to take my hand. "*Bonjour,* Peter. We went ahead and started going over your drawings. Mr. Franklin just showed me your exterior ideas." I glanced over at my boss and received a definite disapproving look, but it was quickly replaced with a smile for Richmond.

"Yes, now you're here, I'll let you show us your preliminary ideas."

I nodded, but before I could begin, Richmond said, "I wanted to ask you if you can join Doris and me for dinner tonight." Then he smiled a mischievous smile. "I believe Mr. Kovachich will be joining us."

I nodded, trying not to give too much of the familiarity away to my prudish boss. "Yes, I ran into Trevor at the park on the way to work this morning. In fact, that's why I was late. He said they were serving scampi."

"Oh great, I love scampi," Richmond said, his smile broadening. He let the subject drop while my boss was in the room.

Luckily, Richmond approved of over eighty percent of my ideas. The only thing he didn't like was the gothic interior. "I like there being some elements that pull you into the neo-Victorian, but it's too dark for a modern shopping experience."

He pointed at the design. "The mahogany columns could be better utilized on the side walls outlining lighted cases, leaving the middle of the rooms just with illuminated shelves. That plays into an open concept while winking at the Victorian design, *oui*?"

I smiled at him. "Yes, it does."

It really was more interesting to work with an artist. They could see things people outside of the creative marketplace couldn't. "We'll also need some signature pieces in the middle of the rooms as separators, but they should all play on the mechanical elements of steampunk."

I was so impressed with this man's vision. As he spoke, I could see the store's layout in my mind.

"That's going to be awesome, Mr. Richmond," I said.

I sat down with my sketchpad and drew out what I was envisioning. As I drew, Richmond and Mr. Franklin chatted. I could only barely make out that Richmond was talking to my boss about Doris and Trevor's home. I did make out Richmond telling Mr.

Franklin that he wanted to host a coming-out party there for the new business. It was going to be like a ribbon-cutting but more elegant.

Mr. Franklin didn't have an elegant bone in his body, and I almost chuckled at the thought of the older man pretending to appreciate Richmond's idea. I could only imagine he was mortified by it.

When I'd finished the drawing, I pushed the notepad over for Richmond to look at. "That's my vision exactly," he said with a huge smile.

"I can get these drawings put together for you over the next few days. You should have some mock-ups for your party provided I get started right away." I turned toward Mr. Franklin and asked, "Do you think I would be able to dedicate my time to this project?" I knew this was the biggest account we had at the moment, and I assumed Mr. Franklin would put everyone on it, but I didn't want to share the project with a lot of people who'd just screw up the finesse I thought this project would need. I knew there'd be hell to pay for putting my boss on the spot like this, but in the long run, it would be worth it.

Mr. Franklin nodded hesitantly. "Yes, I think I can delegate your other projects to your associate architects. Are you confident you can have all the plans written up in time for us to put the models together?"

Here was my payback because now, I was on the hook if the project didn't get completed on time. "I do. It'll require some long hours, but I do think the mock-ups would be a great demonstration piece for the coming-out party."

Richmond sat across from Mr. Franklin and me, absorbing everything we said, then he stood up. "I trust you, Peter. Unless you need more from me, I'm going to take my leave. I wanted to spend some time exploring the Kovachich's neighborhood. I saw several small properties there I'd like to take a look at."

When Richmond left, Mr. Franklin just shook his head. "You've really put a lot of pressure on yourself. But, if anyone can pull this off, it's you. Let me know if you need help. I would've put Fricks on the project with you, but I'm guessing you don't want his help."

My face flushed a bit in spite of myself, and the old man chuckled. "I can't say I blame you. I didn't like to team up when I was your age either, but remember, you need to ask for help if you need it. You're a smart kid, so I'll just trust you." He stood up and continued to talk. "Well, to a point. Come see me Monday morning with what you've gotten done. If you stay on track, I'll let you keep on it, but I warn you, if you fall behind, I'm gonna put Fricks on this with you." He looked me in the eyes. "Got it?"

I nodded, relieved I'd gotten my way.

The rest of the day, I spent deep in the project. When five o'clock came around, I was still so buried I didn't realize what time it was until the main room's lights went dark. Shit, I needed to clean up before going over to the Kovachich's. I finished up a couple ideas I was working on, saved my work, and shut the computer down.

As I left the building, I realized this was probably the only night for weeks that I was going to get out of the office before nine o'clock. I only had myself to blame, but this project was right in my wheelhouse. I loved taking old architectural concepts and adding or taking out elements to make them uber-modern, or in this case, steampunk.

If I played my cards right, maybe this project would lead to more of this type of design work. It was the perfect project for me, and if today was any indication, the inspiration I felt while working on the project kept me glued to the computer.

I rushed home, showered the day off, changed into clean clothes, and rushed over to Trevor's house just in time to hear Luka's loud screeches. Dang, I could hear them all the way to the street. The boy had some remarkable lungs.

When Doris let me into the house, I saw Richmond in the back with eyes the size of saucers. I greeted Doris, then walked into the parlor, where Trevor paced with Luka, trying to calm him.

"Want me to try?" I asked.

"If you want," Trevor sighed.

Unlike last time, Luka didn't calm down as quickly, which was both a disappointment and a relief. I was beginning to wonder if my mom had made some deal with the devil. Something to give me special powers over babies that would increase her chances of grandchildren.

Trevor went into the kitchen and fixed a bottle.

As he walked away from me, he said, "He already had his bottle just an hour ago, but God help us, if we're gonna have any peace, I'm going to have to give him at least a half of another."

Almost the moment Trevor put the bottle up to his mouth, Luka calmed down, although he still hiccupped while sucking, from being so upset.

"Want me to take him now?" Trevor asked.

"No, I like holding him. Why don't you go mingle with Doris and Mr. Richmond? I'll just walk around here while Luka finishes eating."

Trevor looked at me oddly, then put his hand on my forearm and agreed, albeit reluctantly. "We're just in the next room if you need us."

"We'll be fine," I assured him.

When Trevor left, I gazed at the little man in my arms, and like last time, I quietly sang the songs my mom used to sing to me when I was little.

It only took seconds for Luka to finish the partial bottle his father had made him. I expected when he was done, he'd start screaming again, but instead, he looked up at me with those bright blue eyes, kicked his feet, and waved his hands. I grinned at him as I realized he was happy.

"Let's see if you stay happy when I burp you," I said.

I found a cloth diaper sitting next to his bassinet, threw it over my shoulder, and patted his back like I used to do with my little cousins. It only took a couple seconds for him to burp, then I sat down with him and let him lay on my closed legs. I took his cute fingers in my hands and began blowing kisses at him.

"You are cute as a bug, you know that?" I asked him.

He wiggled and kicked his legs as Doris came in. "Wow, I haven't seen him that happy since before he had his shots. Maybe we need more cute men to come visit." She chuckled while watching us.

"Maybe," I said. "Or he just wanted a little more formula, and I'm reaping the benefits of him getting his way?"

"I think you hit the nail on the head," Trevor replied as he came in. "Until Luka, I had no idea an infant could be so demanding. But when this one wants something, he could blow the roof off the house if he doesn't get it."

"Like his dad?" I asked.

Doris laughed out loud. "You learn quick."

Trevor just gave both of us the stink eye but smiled. "His mom was as stubborn as I ever was, so I guess he comes by it naturally."

Doris's face took on a sad expression at the mention of the baby's mom. She didn't say anything about her, instead changing the subject to include Richmond. "I've come to see there are two kinds of men on this earth. Those who are natural with babies, and those who are scared to death of them. I can see which one you are, Peter. Which are you, Leo?"

Richmond squirmed. "I don't have a lot of experience with babies."

Doris laughed out loud. "Don't worry, if it wasn't for my nephews, I doubt I'd ever have been around babies myself." She went over to Richmond and kissed his cheek, and they exchanged a genuine look of affection.

"Is anyone else besides my son hungry tonight?" Trevor asked.

"I'm famished," I admitted. "I haven't eaten all day."

"Good, we have scampi, from the Old World. My grandpa used to say, 'soup and salad.'"

Doris chimed in, "Then we have a very yummy chocolate cake that Leo brought with him. Let's get started."

Trevor came over to take Luka from me, but the moment he picked him up, Luka began to fuss. I stood up and reached out for the baby again, and immediately, he calmed back down.

"Seems my son has a bit of a crush."

I smiled at that. "Well, why should he be left out of the crushes around here?"

Trevor blushed, and so did Doris and Richmond.

I held the baby for most of the night, or at least until he fell asleep on my shoulder. Finally, Trevor took him and laid him in the bassinet, so I was finally able to eat. The scampi was truly out of this world. "I've always loved scampi, but this is different from anything I've eaten before."

"*Oui*, this is very good," Richmond agreed.

"As Trevor said earlier, this is my dad's recipe," Doris explained. "He used to make it for every dinner party, saying everyone who visited needed a taste of the old country since that's who and what we came from."

"You must both have been very close to him," I said.

"He kept the family together," Doris replied, sadness crossing her face. "We both miss him awfully, and he'd have really liked both of you. Leo, he'd have asked a million questions about Paris, and he'd have wanted to know if you ever traveled to Croatia."

Both Doris and Trevor chuckled. "It's pretty much all we'd have talked about for the rest of the night," Trevor said.

Doris jumped up and served each of us a piece of cake while Trevor collected our scampi plates and took them into the kitchen.

As we ate, I couldn't help but ask who redesigned the home, since it was clear it was different from the original design.

"After my mom died, Dad hired a company to come and move things around," Doris explained. "The tiny back kitchen had been Mom's least favorite place in the house, and we never used the library. So he combined the entire back of the house to create a nice-size kitchen."

"It's beautifully designed. Your dad managed to retained its character while the changes modernized it well.

"It's not the modern concept many people want these days," Doris said. "But I agree, I think it's a great compromise between modern living and maintaining the character."

When we'd finished our cake, Doris glanced over at Richmond. "Why don't you boys go take a walk while Leo and I keep an eye on Luka?"

Trevor smirked. "You always volunteer to watch him when he isn't screaming."

"Duh," she said. "Now go away so Leo and I have some time without the kids underfoot."

Trevor gave her a look, making her laugh, but he grabbed my hand and pulled me out the front door. "Beggars can't really be choosers," he said as we walked outside.

When we closed the door behind us, he turned to me. "I haven't been able to think about much except that kiss this morning. Can we try it again to see if it's as amazing when I'm not an emotional train wreck?"

He didn't have to ask me twice. I moved into his arms and took his mouth with mine.

This morning had been toe-curling, but this one was fireworks. God, this man's mouth did strange and wonderful things to my brain.

Trevor

I knew I was being ridiculous, but I couldn't help it. I wanted to feel Peter's mouth on mine again. It was the opposite of what I'd said I wanted this morning, but that was before I'd tasted him and felt those lips attached to mine.

The weather was unusually pleasant for Atlanta this time of year. It was usually way too hot, but tonight we'd opened the windows of the music room to take advantage and air the house out. Apparently, my aunt Doris was going through a romantic streak because the sound of one of my grandpa's old records started drifting through the window. I almost choked when I heard Harry James's orchestral sound that began the song "*It's Been a Long, Long Time.*"

I pulled back just as Kitty Kallen's romantic voice started up. "Never thought that you would be standing here so close to me..." Peter began to sway with the music as he held me. "Kiss me once, then kiss me twice, then kiss me once again. It's been a long, long time..."

I'll never forget the sly smile crossing his beautiful face. As we swayed with the music, he leaned down and kissed me like it was me singing the song to him.

I know its cliché, but I couldn't help but think how my smaller frame fit so perfectly against his larger one. As Harry James's trumpet pierced the air, Peter swirled me out and then back in for a final kiss. This one was much more intense.

As Ella and Louis's "*Dream a Little Dream of Me,*" replaced James and Kallen, Peter continued to swing with me on the front porch. "Did you set that up?" he asked.

I smiled. "No, but it sure fits me."

"Me too," he admitted.

We continued to dance to the old musical ballads. I chuckled when Louis's voice belted out, *"Heaven, I'm in heaven."*

"This is almost too perfect," I said.

"Indeed," Peter said as we began to move to the faster pace of the music. "I haven't really heard these songs outside a movie," he admitted.

I chuckled. "My grandpa played these records all the time. It was as much a part of my childhood as this old home was."

"I'm jealous of your childhood," Peter said.

I laughed but with little mirth. "Don't be too jealous. I have shit for parents."

"But it sounds like you had the best alternative," he said.

I pulled in closer to him, as Ella sang about dancing cheek to cheek. I did as she instructed.

Peter looked down at me and kissed me again.

I laid my head on his chest as we swayed with the rhythm.

We stayed like that for several moments until I heard someone stomping up the steps.

"Let that man go!" I heard him say before I recognized who was there.

I pulled away from Peter and looked square in the face of my father. My mom stood only steps behind him.

I reacted before I thought about what to say. "Who the hell are you to come here and tell me to stop doing something?"

My father's reaction was swift. He grabbed me by the collar and was about to hit me when Peter's big hand came around and lifted my dad up and away from me.

"Sir, you need to vacate the premises right now before I do something you'll regret," he said to my father.

By this time, my aunt and Leonardo were coming out of the front door.

My aunt looked at my father as he dangled above the ground, then at my mom. Without addressing him, she asked my mom, "Rita, why are you here?"

My mother angrily responded, "Can't I come over to my own father's house?"

Aunt Doris turned toward my dad and put her hand on Peter's arm, encouraging him to let him down. "Not when you bring this man with you," she said while looking my father in the eye.

My father was still stunned at being manhandled by Peter. I'm sure in his mind all gay men were pansies that he could bully. Being forcefully removed from me must have really shocked him and stung his pride.

Obviously surprised that my father hadn't responded, my mother came to his defense. "I can see this place is just as full of sin as it ever was. Edward, I'll wait for you in the car."

My father regained his senses and said under his breath, "You stay right there, Rita. I want you to witness this." Pointing toward me, he said, "You are no son of mine, you little faggot. You stay the fuck away from us from now on, you hear?"

I felt Peter tense next to me, but I put my hand on his to stop him from reacting.

"That's the best gift you've ever given me," I responded. "I'll say the same to you. You aren't now and never have been my parents. From this point forward, I want nothing to do with you. Please leave this property and never return."

This clearly shocked my father. He'd always known me as a quiet, meek child. I'd learned early in life to avoid making him angry, knowing the slightest infraction could turn violent. But something about having Peter next to me, and knowing my son was less than a few feet away from us, made me feel confident and stronger than I ever had before.

I could see out of the corner of my eye that Aunt Doris was crying, and I wanted to comfort her. I knew the inevitable separation was hurting her more than it ever would me, but the danger hadn't passed. My father was a violent man, and now that he'd been confronted, he was unpredictable.

There was a sort of standoff as we all stood facing each other until Peter put his arm around me, showing a united front against the foe.

"You'll all rot in hell soon enough," my father said. Then he turned to leave. He grabbed my mom roughly as he walked past her and pulled her along with him. It was dark enough in the shadows that I was unsure what her reaction to all this was, but truth be told I didn't really give a damn what she thought any longer.

Unfortunately, it was at that moment that Luka let out a wail. My mother turned out of my father's hands and said, "So, it's true?"

I ignored her and turned to go inside to tend to my son.

I was done with my parents. Hopefully, for the rest of my life. At the moment, I'd rather change a million nasty diapers than spend one more minute with the shit show that they were.

Aunt Doris, Peter, and Leonardo followed close behind me, and I heard the door shut as I walked toward Luka's bassinet.

I took Luka to the bathroom, where the changing table was, and changed him. When I came back, Peter, Leonardo, and Aunt Doris were all sitting in the parlor. The music we'd been so thoroughly enjoying before my parents had shown up was turned off, and the room was silent.

"I'm sorry for the theatrics out there, but this has been coming to a head for some time. They usually avoid us and this place like the plague," I said as I glanced over at my aunt, then at Peter. "I'm not sure why they picked tonight to come by."

Peter smiled. "As you know, we can't control what our family does. Hell, mine even hired a private investigator to track down my ex."

I wouldn't have thought it possible after the horror of what my parents had just put us through, but Peter actually made me laugh.

"Your mom is a handful, no doubt, but at least she loves you."

Peter sighed. "That's true. And your aunt loves you," he said as he glanced over at Aunt Doris.

Tears spilled from her eyes, and she stood up, pulling me into a hug. "I didn't know they'd stoop this low. Dad forbade them to come to the house unless they let us know they were coming first. I guess since he passed, they thought they could ignore that rule."

"Clearly," I huffed.

"Anyway, I'm glad this is done and over with. I'm just sorry Peter and Leonardo had to witness it."

"Don't apologize for me," Leonardo said. "Family is unpredictable. France and England have been at war since the Romans left centuries ago. Since I'm both British and French, you can imagine the drama between the two families."

We all chuckled.

I looked over at Peter. "Thanks for coming to my rescue. I'm guessing I'd have gotten a good beating if it hadn't been for you."

Peter's expression was somber. "You should consider getting a restraining order against him."

"Not very likely to happen here in Atlanta," I replied. "He's an upstanding member of the community, and there is no evidence he ever did anything violent to me. My mom talked my grandpa into not pressing charges when he broke my arm."

Peter didn't reply and looked down at his hands.

Doris wiped her eyes and stood. "I think we all need another glass of wine and maybe another slice of cake. We don't have to let their childishness ruin the entire evening."

Leonardo smiled up at her. "I'll help," he said, and they both left the room.

"Thank you," I said again as I bobbed the now sleeping Luka in my arms.

"I could've beaten him to a pulp," Peter replied. "I'm glad your aunt came out when she did because I thought he was just some homophobe who'd been walking down the street. I came really close to decking your father."

"He isn't my father. He was a sperm donor, that's it. My real father was Luka Kovachich, my biological grandfather. And my real mom has been my aunt Doris. Those two people out there really are nothing to me. They haven't been for a long time."

"Is that why you use your grandfather's last name?" Peter asked.

I nodded. "Yeah, I legally changed it when I turned eighteen, but I've used their name since I was ten."

Peter stood up and moved around me and Luka, giving us a hug from behind.

"My mom adores you, so you give the word, and I'm one hundred percent sure she'd adopt you. The way she talks about you, I think she might already have."

I laughed as I snuggled into Peter's warm embrace. "She'd be pretty awesome as long as she doesn't have a brain tumor."

Peter chuckled. "She doesn't really manage those very well."

"Apparently," I agreed.

We stayed like that until Aunt Doris and Leonardo came in with the cake and wine.

We spent the rest of the evening chatting companionably, but the heaviness of the earlier events still plagued us.

When Leonardo left, Aunt Doris walked him out. "I should be going, too," Peter said. "I'm pulling extra shifts to get his project done before the party. I'll be working way too much. Can I plan to come over next weekend? If I don't plan ahead, I'm afraid I'll never be able to see you."

I smiled. "That sounds great. I'll see if Aunt Doris can watch Luka."

"No need," Peter replied, surprising me. "Let's go do something where we can bring him with us."

"Sounds good," I agreed. "But just so you know, that means we'll need to do something in the morning. Anything after his noon bottle means he'll be grumpy. He's a total homebody after lunch."

"How about Saturday morning for breakfast at the diner?"

"The Lisa diner?"

"Unless it's uncomfortable for you."

"No, that's perfect, actually. At least we know we'll have plenty of privacy as the wait staff pass Luka around."

"Exactly, it'll be fun for all three of us."

I laughed again and leaned into Peter for a kiss. "Thank you for tonight. I really enjoyed watching the old man's face when you lifted him off his feet."

Peter smiled. "Next time, can I hit him?"

"We'll see," I replied.

Peter kissed me again and walked toward the door. "See you next Saturday," he said and was gone.

I sat down just as the tears fell from my face. I held them while Leonardo and Peter were around, but they'd been threatening to spill over since I'd tossed the two hateful fuckers out of my life for good. Not that I was crying for them. No, those tears dried up long ago. I cried because I knew how much Aunt Doris and Grandpa had hoped my mom would come to her senses, and that I would one day reconnect with her and she'd become a real mom.

I knew that wasn't ever going to happen, but I'd let their hopes and dreams be mine, and now, I was finally free of them. The feeling was both bittersweet and overwhelming. And, for my aunt, sad.

She came in and sat on the settee with me, laying her head on my shoulder. "I'm sorry," she said.

"For what? It wasn't your fault," I replied.

"No, but I'm sorry anyway."

"Aunt Doris, I told you, they don't mean anything to me. I really just want them both out of my life for good. I know that's tough for you to hear because Rita is your sister, but they've always been bad juju for me. I feel freer now than I ever have. I just wish Peter and Leonardo hadn't been pulled into the middle of it."

Aunt Doris looked up. "I thank God that Peter was here," she said. "I can't imagine the damage that asshole would've done had he not been."

"That's true. I can defend myself in most situations, but I doubt I'd have fought back... too many years being trained to cower down to him."

"I'll call Rita tomorrow. Tell her she's no longer welcome here, and if we see them anywhere near the property, we'll have Dad's attorney draw up papers for a restraining order. Like you, I think there aren't any judges in Atlanta that'd grant one against your father.

But they're so concerned with appearances I'm guessing the threat may be enough."

I side hugged her since I was still holding Luka, and she leaned over to kiss my cheek. "I love you, sweet boy," she said with tears filling her eyes again.

"I know, Aunt Doris. I love you, too!"

She got up then and reached for Luka. "Let me have him. I'll get him ready for bed. That'll give you a few minutes to yourself. I can imagine you need them."

I smiled and let her take Luka from me.

The moment he was out of my arms, I immediately felt vulnerable. Like someone had snatched my heart out of my body.

Luka had become my center, my reason for living. Even the events of the evening and telling my parents they were no longer welcome in my life felt insignificant as long as he was mine to love. Luka filled the gap where my parents should've existed. He filled my heart in places even the intense and unconditional love my grandpa and aunt hadn't been able to fill.

I went upstairs and washed my face and changed into the t-shirt and shorts I usually slept in.

When I came back out, Aunt Doris was putting the conked-out Luka in his bed. She came over to me and gave me a proper hug. "I'm so proud of you," she whispered. "You were so strong tonight. Your grandpa would've been proud, too."

I'm not sure why that caused me to feel weepy, but it did. I hugged her back as the two of us held onto each other like people who'd lost someone important to them tended to do.

When we pulled back, Aunt Doris kissed my cheek and wished me a goodnight. I doubted I'd sleep much, but at least I felt like something important had happened, and a door that had been letting in bad energy had finally been closed.

"Goodnight," I said as she left my room.

I lay in bed and stared at Luka sleeping for what felt like hours. I was surprised when I woke up and found the little one staring back at me. I swear this little person had some ability to know when he was needed. We stared at each other until Luka began to stir. I grabbed his bottle from the small refrigerator I kept in my room and warmed it up in the nearby microwave while he watched me.

"I love you so much," I told him. "You will never, ever feel like I don't want you with all my heart. I'm here for you night and day, winter or summer, no matter what!"

Luka grunted like he'd understood deep down. I think he probably had.

The tears flowed from my eyes again and not for the first time in my life, I thanked God my grandpa and aunt had taught me what unconditional love felt like, so I knew how to give that to my little man.

After I burped him and changed his diaper, he fell right back to sleep, and when I laid him down this time, I did as well. I wasn't thinking about my horrible birth parents, but rather about how much love I felt for my family, my real family... which included a particularly grumpy infant son.

Peter

I didn't get to spend nearly enough time with Trevor and Luka as I'd have liked. We continued to hit snags with the project. That meant I spent most days working late into the evening. I ended up working from home most days, spending at least sixteen hours a day on the project and even forgetting to eat. But the more snags I found, the happier I was to work through the challenge.

Unfortunately, halfway into the project, I had to accept help. But luckily, my boss put a college intern on the project since Fricks had his hands full. She and I were able to pull together most of the issues.

By the third week, we'd completed enough of the plans that we could make the models for the party. I reached out to Trevor to see if Doris could keep Luka for the evening so he could come out and celebrate with me.

I pulled into his driveway to pick him up and almost drooled when he walked down the steps to meet me. He was dressed in a tight pair of jeans and a black shirt. Damn, how could someone look that hot in jeans and a t-shirt? I always saw him in casual, loose-fitting t-shirts and jeans. He was hot in those but the way his shirt outlined his abs and God help me, I couldn't wait until he turned around so I could see how those jeans shaped his bubble butt.

Dang, I had it bad. But who wouldn't with this man?

When he climbed in, I almost swooned. He was wearing a soft fragrance, something I didn't recognize. But shit if it wasn't sexy as hell! I couldn't help myself. I leaned over and nuzzled his neck. "Damn, you smell nice," I said.

Trevor chuckled sexily, and the sound went right to my groin.

"Can we skip everything, and I just take you to my condo?" I asked, only half teasing.

Trevor glanced over at me after I pulled back, and the expression on his face wasn't humor. "I want to say yes, but I'm not sure that's a good idea."

"I think it's the best idea I've ever had, but I'm not going to push. My friend Joshua is already at the bar. He wants to meet you in person. I've told him so much about you that he thinks I'm lying. 'No one is that perfect,'" I mimicked him saying.

Trevor laughed at me. "Then you better stop looking at me like you did when I got in and absolutely no more nuzzling my neck. That's my weak spot."

I felt myself growl. "You know, Joshua may need some alone time!"

Trevor pushed me back when I went in for the second nuzzle. "Nope," he laughed. "Joshua first. I want to meet him, too."

I leaned back and readjusted myself since the front of my pants had immediately gotten a lot tighter. "If you say so," I replied suddenly, wishing Joshua would take a flying leap.

"How long before you have to be back?" I asked, trying to be all innocent.

Trevor laughed at me again. "Not long enough, I'm afraid."

I sighed and put the car into drive. "We need to plan a whole night out. I'll pay for a nanny if I have to!"

Trevor

I regretted that we couldn't just go to Peter's place. When he nuzzled my neck, I almost came on myself. It'd been way too long since I'd been touched. Shit, it was months before I became a single parent. Luckily, Peter had a friend waiting on us, or I would have just jumped on him then and there. That was a really bad idea. I needed to stay focused. No fooling around at least until Luka was a little older, and I could afford to leave him with a sitter.

When we got to the bar, we approached a guy sitting with his back to us.

"You absolutely look like a fish out of water," Peter said as we came up behind him.

"You are late," he said as he turned around. He blushed when he saw me. "Sorry, Peter and I have an ongoing argument about punctuality. The guy doesn't seem to own a watch."

I laughed. "I hadn't noticed that yet. Hi, I'm Trevor," I said, saving Peter from having to introduce us.

"I'm Joshua," he said.

"Yes, Joshua, heaven forbid you ever call him Josh!" Peter said playfully and got a nasty look from his friend.

Ignoring Peter, Joshua turned to the server who'd just come up behind us. "We're all here."

The restaurant wasn't busy, so we were taken to our table right away.

"What do you do?" I asked Joshua.

"I work in construction," he replied. "Well, I work for my dad, who owns a construction company."

"Cool, so that's how you two know each other?"

Peter smiled. "I met Joshua when I came to Atlanta. His father hired me after Martin and I split up."

"You two dated, right?" I asked.

Peter laughed. "Yep, and that's why I no longer work for Joshua's dad."

"Yeah, you mentioned that," I replied. "And the two of you didn't work out?" I was trying to figure out what was going on between these two.

"Oh no... not even a little," Joshua replied. "We make great friends, but we really failed at everything else."

Peter laughed again. "Truth... that's the absolute truth."

I couldn't help it. I had to push. "So, why did you fail so bad?"

Peter smiled at me. "Fishing for details, are we?"

"Maybe." I returned his smile. "Inquiring minds and all that."

Joshua chimed in then. "Well, after my dad fired him, he was stuck on the unemployment line, and that didn't do much for our relationship. Then we found we were anything but compatible, and, to be honest, kissing him was, well, for me, it was like kissing my best friend."

Peter turned toward his friend. "The light just didn't come on."

"Perfectly stated," Joshua replied.

"We are and will always be best friends. That's just all we are."

Peter smiled and looked back at me. "Besides, he doesn't react the same way when I kiss his neck."

I blushed and decided to change the subject before things got embarrassing.

Joshua was charming, and I enjoyed hanging with him. It only took a few minutes before I could see the two really weren't compatible and used their differences as tools to enhance a genuine friendship. I couldn't find it in me to be jealous of the man, especially since he came across as mostly sad and more than a little lonely.

We had several drinks before Joshua announced he needed to get home. "Congratulations on getting that project done," he told Peter.

"It was really nice to meet you, Trevor," Joshua said before he stood to leave. "Let's get together again. I'd like to meet the little one, too. Peter talks about him about as much as he does you."

Peter blushed, and I chuckled. "That's good to know," I said as I turned to Peter.

"Yep, time to go, Joshua," he said, causing both of us to laugh.

"I'll talk to you later, Joshua. Seems we have a lot more to talk about. Maybe we'll get together when Peter's not around?"

"Hey, you're going to make me jealous," Peter said, but he stood and pulled Joshua into a hug. "Take care, and don't let your dad get to you, OK?"

"Easier said than done," Joshua replied with a frown but bounced back quickly. "Y'all have a good night, and don't do anything I wouldn't do." He winked at us before turning to go.

We watched him leave, and I put my hand over Peter's. "You care a lot about him, don't you?"

"Yeah," he admitted. "His dad is a total jackass. Ain't worth shit as a parent. I just wish Joshua would tell him to fuck himself and get away from him."

"Yeah, that's easier said than done," I replied.

Peter turned to me and sighed. "Yeah, I forgot you have some experience with that?"

"Too much, as you know all too well."

"Has he tried to contact you again?"

"Oh no, that's not my dad's M.O.," I replied. "He's more the sneaky, get-you-while-you-aren't-looking type."

"Are you afraid he'll try something?"

"Oh, he'll eventually try something, but I doubt I'm in any danger. He values his reputation more than anything else, so he won't take any chances on getting a restraining order. Especially one from his son."

"He didn't seem too concerned that night," Peter replied, worry lines stretching across his face.

"Well, that's because when he saw us dancing in public, it was a threat to his identity as well. I'm sure he's terrified someone will find out I'm bisexual."

Peter sighed. "I never really knew my dad. My mother always told me she was sure he'd be accepting of me, and my grandparents on his side certainly were before they passed away."

"Same with my grandpa. He was one hundred percent cool, as was Aunt Doris. I always wondered what the hell happened to my mother."

"Sounds like your dad happened," he said, and I couldn't disagree.

"OK, change of subject. We've given them enough of our time. Let's talk about something interesting."

"Like that sensitive area, you mentioned earlier?"

Peter looked me in the eye, and I all but melted in my seat.

"You aren't playing fair... you know I'm a desperate housewife!"

Peter's grin turned feral. "How desperate?"

That expression sent chills up my spine. "Too desperate... way too desperate!"

"Let's get out of here, and you can show me!" he replied, the raw, lustful expression still clearly present on his face.

Luckily, we'd already paid our bill because the speed at which we left the restaurant left no time for either of us to think about such things.

Peter grabbed me when we got to the car and pushing my back against the door, he pulled me into a full-on kiss. I have never thrown caution to the wind like I did when in Peter's presence. I tended to be discreet, but this guy did something to my insides that made me forget all that and instead focus only on the lustful needs he seemed to bring out in me.

We managed to climb into his car, and as we drove toward his place, I let my hand rub his thigh. I could see his hard-on through his pants, and I wondered how brave I was. I'd never been this forward with a guy. Hell, I'd only been with a couple of guys and those were very... *wham, bam, thank you ma'am.*

I decided to throw caution to the wind and let my hand rub over the bump in his jeans. Peter almost lost control of the car, and I pulled back, laughing. "You are easy to distract."

"Well, yeah, when you do that, I am!"

Luckily, Peter didn't live far from where we'd met Joshua. When we pulled into his parking lot, he threw the car into park, jumped out, and was at my door all but pulling me out of the passenger seat.

Once again, he pushed me up against the car and kissed me passionately, driving his tongue into my mouth. I was so desperate for him at this point, I could hardly breathe. Peter pulled back and unceremoniously dragged me up the stairs to the front door of his condo.

Under normal circumstances, I think I'd have wanted to see where I was, maybe tour the place where Peter lived, but tonight, all I could think of was his skin touching mine.

Peter was the one pushing us up until that point. But the moment we were in his bedroom, and he removed his shirt, all that changed. I wanted my hands on him, I wanted my mouth and tongue on him, and I didn't let ceremony get in my way.

I jerked my shirt off and pushed Peter onto his bed. I straddled him, letting my tongue make its way from his mouth down to his perfectly formed nipples that hardened with my touch.

I was hungry for him, and his moans just spurred me on. I came back up and nibbled on his delicious, muscular neck, and my tongue moved along the hard muscles that tensed for me there. I felt my dick strain against my jeans, knowing I'd have a nice wet spot there when I finally freed it.

Peter grabbed me, turned me over, and climbed on top, letting his crotch grind into mine as he nuzzled the place on my neck that I'd told him earlier was one of my erogenous zones.

"Oh God!" he exclaimed. "This area right here is all I could think of all night. Poor Joshua sat across from me, but my mind couldn't focus on anything but this." Peter licked my neck, then sucked on it. I was sure I was going to have a hickey if he sucked much harder, but for the life of me, I couldn't have stopped him even if I'd wanted to. And I sure as hell didn't want to stop him.

My dick was so hard it hurt. Peter reached down between us and unbuttoned my jeans, and I all but sighed with relief as my cock was freed from its constraint. He jumped off the bed and pulled my jeans off. He then proceeded to remove his own before climbing back on. Peter ground our underwear-clad bodies against each other, sucking on my neck, nibbling and sending chills all down my body.

Peter

Trevor's body was perfect, everything I'd fantasized it would be. Lean but muscular chest, slight but accented abs. His lithe form was beautiful to look at and even more wonderful to touch.

I loved the way he squirmed as I nibbled and sucked on his neck. He wasn't joking when he said that was one of his most erogenous areas, and I was going to take full advantage of that knowledge.

I was determined to mark him, put myself there, so the rest of the world would know he's mine. His body was mine to possess. For a moment, I drew back. I'd never thought like that before. Hell, I always thought that kind of attitude was cavemanish, but something about Trevor caused me to revert to caveman-like tendencies.

When I could tell he was utterly lost in lust, I moved my mouth down his perfect body until I was sucking his cock through his underwear.

"Oh God, Peter, oh God!" he exclaimed, and I smiled inwardly. I was going to show this man everything I had to give tonight. I pulled his underwear down, and his perfect cock slapped his stomach.

"Wow, you were hiding the prize in there!" I said, surprised at his size.

Trevor looked down, and panic crossed his face. "Too much?" he asked, and I laughed out loud.

"You don't have much experience with gay men, do you? I'm not sure it's ever enough."

Trevor smiled, pulled me up to his mouth, and kissed me. "I'm not worried about other gay men, I'm worried about you, the man I'm currently having mind-blowing sex with."

I laughed again. "No, it's not too much. It's perfect... you're perfect. Now, if you don't mind, I was busy doing something I'd like to return to."

When I went back down on him and took his cock in my mouth, Trevor all but sighed, "Oh *God*, nope... don't mind! Don't mind at all!"

If I didn't have a mouth full of cock, I'm sure I'd have laughed, but no way was I going to let him go now that I had him in my mouth. I let my lips caress his head, sucking while licking his slit. Trevor's moans egged me on.

When I finally took his shaft, thrusting his head deep into my throat, Trevor arched. "Damn, I'm going to come too soon! Peter, I'm coming!"

Fuck, fuck, fuck! I said to myself as that gorgeous cock unloaded into my throat. I swear I almost choked on the amount of cum.

When he'd finished emptying himself in my mouth, I pulled off him and licked up any remainder. I moved back up and nuzzled his neck while he finished convulsing with pleasure.

"Fuck," he finally said. "Fuck, I needed that!"

I smiled at him. "Yeah, me too." Then I laid my head on his beautiful chest and let myself enjoy just being on top of him, holding and touching him after only being able to fantasize about it until now.

I was just about to drift off when Trevor stirred underneath me.

His hands began to massage my shoulders and head, then he moved me onto my back and began kissing me again.

"My turn," he mumbled as he kissed his way down my chest and torso.

Trevor

God, it felt so good to come in Peter's mouth. I didn't have it in me to tell him I was totally kinked out by cum and would've rather he had kissed me than cuddle, but that was totally OK. I wasn't going to miss my opportunity.

The thought of his cock in my mouth drove me to skip all the other foreplay and go right for the part of him I'd fantasized about since the night we'd danced on my front porch.

I quickly pulled his underwear off and took his cock into my mouth. Peter wasn't as big as me, for which I was thankful. I couldn't imagine dealing with a huge cock. I'd fantasized about being fucked, and I was self-conscious about being too big for any normal man, or woman for that matter. The last time I fucked someone was Lisa, and both of us had been seriously drunk. Otherwise, I doubt it would've gone very far.

I was obsessed with tasting Peter, and I set to sucking him so he'd come sooner than later.

Peter groaned as I thrust his cock into my mouth, then tongued the edges of his head and slit, just as he'd done to me moments before.

I knew where the sensitive areas were on my own cock, and I made sure to hit those areas as I mouth fucked him.

Peter arched and moved under me before he finally grabbed my head, pulling me up to him, kissing me, then pushing me onto my back.

He straddled my face, then began fucking my mouth. Oh my God, that was the hottest thing I'd ever experienced. I loved the aggressiveness of the move. I liked feeling his cock being driven forcefully into my mouth, almost gagging me as it hit the back of my throat. Peter would pull almost out and tease me with his head before thrusting himself into my mouth again.

All I could do was moan with pleasure as this man took me again and again.

I could occasionally see beyond his torso to his face, which was flush with pleasure as he pumped into me.

Finally, his face contorted, and he moaned loudly. Without warning, he came in my mouth, pouring himself into me, fucking me through his orgasm. His salty seed filled my senses, and for the first time in my life, I knew I preferred the taste of a man over most other things on earth.

When he was done, Peter pulled off me, bending down and taking my mouth with his.

Oh fuck yeah, that was the hottest thing *ever*! Again, I knew I had a cum kink, and apparently, so did Peter, who was kissing me with great gusto.

When Peter pulled back, he let his tongue trail across my lips. He caught my bottom lip in his teeth before gently biting, then letting go.

He fell on his back next to me and sighed.

"I would apologize for being aggressive and all that, but it seems you liked it as much as I did," he said.

"Maybe more," I sighed.

Peter leaned up on his elbow and looked at me with a smile.

"You liked that?" he asked. "Not too kinky?"

"Oh, hell no! Nowhere near too kinky!"

"Good," he replied and fell back onto the bed. "I can't wait to do it again."

I laughed. "You'll have to wait, I'm afraid. I'm going to have to get back home, unfortunately."

"Yeah, I know..." Peter sighed. "You know, maybe Luka can spend the night sometime in the future. That way, you won't have to go home."

I sighed. "That probably isn't a good idea."

I started getting up when Peter pushed me back onto the bed.

"Why not?" he asked. "It's not like I haven't had a baby in my home before. Hell, my cousins used to stay with us all the time."

I sighed again. "Well, Luka isn't one for being out at night. He barely tolerates being in his own home. You could probably just stay with us."

"I'm sure your aunt would be thrilled with that."

I chuckled. "She can go spend the night somewhere else. She knows I'm human. Besides, she often stays out late, and sometimes even all night."

"Good, then let's plan that sooner than later."

I tried to smile. "Peter, I don't know about all that. Luka is so little, and he wakes up at least three times a night, sometimes he doesn't sleep at all. You staying over sounds fun, but in reality, it would be anything but romantic."

I climbed out of bed and started dressing. Peter crawled out of bed and stood behind me. "Oh, I'm sure we'd find ways to make it good for both of us. Does Luka sleep better during the day?"

I thought for a moment. "Yeah, he sleeps best in the afternoon, which is why he doesn't do well when we go somewhere at that time."

"Maybe I just need to come keep you company some afternoon."

I moaned when Peter began sucking on my neck and ran his hands underneath the shirt I'd just put on.

"You drive a hard bargain," I said between moans.

"Good," he replied between neck kisses.

"You have to stop. I really do need to get back home to relieve Aunt Doris of baby duty. She said she has an early morning at the shop."

Peter sighed and moved to where his clothes had been tossed and started pulling on his underwear.

When we were dressed, he took my hand in his and led me out of his condo toward the car. As he drove me back to the house, he held my hand. He occasionally moved it to his mouth to kiss and steal a glance my way.

He pulled into my driveway, leaned over, and kissed me passionately. "I can't wait to do that again, Trevor," he said. "No way am I going to let this be a one-time thing, I have so many plans for what I want to do with your body."

The way he looked at me sent chills up my spine and caused me to get hard again. "Yeah, me too," I managed to squeak out before almost leaping out of the car, knowing if I didn't get away soon, I was going to do some of those things right here in his car. The thought of my parents jumping out of the bushes as I did nasty things to Peter's body was enough to kill the buzz!

"I'll text you tomorrow, and we can make some plans. Deal?"

Peter stared at me and nodded.

I shut the car door and rushed onto the porch, turning only for a second to wave at him before going through the front door.

I'd had several flings with guys before, and most were a one-night thing. But with him, I'd be damned if this was one of those. No, I wanted that man as many ways as I could have him... just when and where was the problem.

Peter

Richmond announced on the Monday following my date with Trevor that he'd purchased the plot for his Atlanta store. I wasn't that surprised when he told me he decided to place the property in Inman Park, close to a trendy new shopping area called the Old Krog Street Market.

Now that the spot had been found, a new level of work would begin on the project. Luckily, much of it would fall to associates in the company.

With most of my part of the project done, my boss gave his blessing to let me start helping out with the party, knowing it would get international attention for our firm.

At first, Trevor was shy around me, not sure how to act after we'd had our amazing suck off. Unfortunately, there wasn't much time when he and I were alone, which made it tough on both of us.

On the first weekend working together on the party, Richmond took Doris out. That was our moment. As soon as Luka was tucked in, I came over and gave Trevor a neck rub.

"Not in here," Trevor said. "Luka will be fine for a couple hours. I made up the guest room next door, so I can hear him if he cries."

I smiled. "You were preparing for us?"

"At this point in my life, if I don't prepare, nothing is going to happen."

I followed Trevor into the room next door, came up behind him and began nuzzling his neck.

"Oh God," he moaned. "You're all I've been able to think about, Peter."

I chuckled as I sucked. "Same here," I replied. "Now strip!"

"Aye, aye, Captain," he responded and began stripping out of his clothes.

I did the same. Both of us hurried, wanting to take advantage of the limited time we had together. Trevor undressed in front of me and immediately fell to his knees and fondled my cock as I struggled the rest of the way out of my pants.

"Fuck, Trevor..."

He moaned as he took my cock into his mouth. "You taste so good, I can't wait to taste your cum again!" he said as he moved my cock in and out.

I raked my hand through his hair while enjoying the sensation of being sucked. "Damn Trevor, you're good at this!" I managed to breathe out.

Trevor got up and laid on the bed with his head hanging slightly off to the side. "Fuck my mouth again, like you did last time."

The thought of that made my cock jump, and I moved over to him, slipping my cock into his mouth. I fucked him, letting him get used to the feel of me inside his mouth before getting too aggressive. When Trevor moaned and his cock grew harder, I fucked his hot mouth, pushing my head into the back of his throat.

I was surprised he didn't gag as I rode him hard. When his own precum slipped out of his slit, I almost shot my load right then. I leaned down to lick the jizz off him. God, he tasted so damned good.

I continued fucking his mouth but sucked his enormous cock into my mouth, putting us into a sixty-nine position. Trevor moaned louder, pushing me to pound his mouth while aggressively sucking his cock.

I pulled off him and jumped on the bed next to him. "Your turn. Fuck my mouth with that giant cock."

Trevor looked hesitant. "You sure?"

"Fuck, Trevor. Yeah, I'm more than sure. I want to taste you while your cock fills me."

Trevor smiled, and when I laid back, he slipped his cock hesitantly into my mouth. *Fuck this*, I thought, and grabbed his hips, taking him into my mouth until the head of his cock hit my throat.

I'd never sucked a cock as big as his, and I didn't know if I could take it, but the feel of him sent me into overdrive. After a moment, he stopped hesitating and slowly began fucking me. I used his hips to force him to fuck my mouth harder and harder. The big shaft filled my mouth.

"Oh, oh!" Trevor moaned until he finally got into the heat of the moment and pounded me as hard as I wanted him to.

"Mmm!" His cock rocked down my throat, and I had to breathe between thrusts.

"I'm gonna come," he said just as he unloaded.

I'm glad I'd already taken a breath. Otherwise, I would've probably choked. The man came like a racehorse.

When he'd finally finished, he leaned down and kissed me. "God, that was hot."

I rose up and sat next to him on the bed. "You ever been fucked?" I asked.

"Once."

"Did you like it?"

"Yeah, but I was too tight, and it hurt." His expression was shy. I was about to suggest we do something else, but then Trevor pushed me back on the bed and straddled me. "I want to try it again, but can you be patient with me?" he asked.

"Yeah..." I managed to squeak.

He chuckled as he lay down on top of me and ground his semi-hard cock on mine.

I rolled him over. "Let me get you ready."

His eyes grew wider. "How?" he asked.

I looked at him in surprise. "You don't know?"

Trevor blushed under me. "I've watched porn, but I haven't had much done to me."

"Oh, then this is going to be fun!" I said with a laugh.

Trevor cocked an eyebrow at me but smiled. "OK."

"Do you trust me?"

Trevor nodded.

"Then lay back and let me take care of you."

I kissed his lips before moving down his gorgeous body and kissing around his cock, getting him hard again. I asked him to lift his legs, and as I gently sucked him, I let my spit-covered fingers slowly massage his hole.

"Oh, fuck!" he moaned.

"Feel good?" I whispered.

"Mmm!" was all he uttered.

I reached over and poured some of the lube he'd pulled out of the nightstand onto my fingers and used that to prep him.

"Tell me if it hurts, and I'll stop, OK?"

Trevor was watching my every move, and although he appeared nervous, he nodded.

I lubed up my hand and jacked him off until he was arching under my movements.

When he thrust his cock into my hand, I pressed one finger into his hole. "Oh fuck, that feels so good," he moaned.

I smiled, knowing he'd probably done this much to himself before.

When I pressed my second finger into him, I put his hand on his cock and reached up to kiss him. "Jack yourself off and press down on my fingers."

He closed his eyes, doing as I asked, and before long, he was riding my fingers as I moved them in and out. When the ecstasy overtook him, I scissored my fingers inside him to prep him further. His moans grew more exaggerated, and the sound of his pleasure caused my own cock to pulsate. I moved between his legs and used my thumb to massage his taint and added a third finger, moving in and out as his moans grew louder and louder.

"God you are so hot, Trevor. I want to be inside you!"

"Yes," he whispered. "Fuck me, Peter!"

He didn't need to ask twice. I ripped open the condom also found in the nightstand and rolled it on while I watched him jack himself off. My cock was so hard it all but vibrated inside the condom.

I lifted his legs, pushed a pillow under him, and slipped my cock into his ass. I was thicker than my three fingers, so I didn't want to overwhelm him. I slowly moved just my head in and out of his hole.

"Is that OK?" I asked, worried I was too much for him.

"No, damn it! Put your cock in me now!" he growled, causing me to chuckle.

While pushing inside him, Trevor arched back into me. I slowly moved inside him until he was begging me to push harder. "Peter, I need it all... give me all your cock," he panted.

I pushed until my shaft was all the way in, and when I could see it wasn't hurting him, I pulled back and let myself push inside him again.

"Fuck, that's perfect. Fuck yeah!" he moaned as his ass loosened around me to allow me in again.

"Your ass is so fucking tight, Trevor!" I said, forcing myself not to pound him like I wanted to.

I leaned up and kissed him while I let him get used to my invasion.

I moved in and out several more times. Reassured he wasn't feeling pain, I let my body take the rhythm it so desperately wanted.

Trevor

I don't know what got into me, but feeling Peter's cock deep inside me made me want to be ridden like I'd never experienced before. I pushed him back, surprising him, but when I kissed him and said, "I want it like this," I got on my knees and pulled a towel I'd laid on the bed under me to catch any cum.

Peter rubbed his hand over my back and ass, then stuck his thumb in my asshole as I began to moan. When I was loose enough again, he moved his cock back in place and slipped inside. The sensation of being fucked from behind was more intense than anything I'd ever experienced before. Peter moved in and out slowly, again getting me used to the invasion, and slowly picking up the rhythm.

"Fuck, you feel so good, Trevor. So fucking tight," he moaned behind me.

"Fuck me harder, Peter!" I said at last, no longer able to stand the slow pace he was setting.

Peter thrust inside me, and every nerve ending in my body went off at the same time. "Oh God, that's right! Fuck me!" I cried.

Peter pounded me harder and harder, and all I wanted was more of him. He shifted at one point, and when he did, his cock hit my prostate, and I saw stars. "Oh fuck!" was all I could say before I lost the ability to say anything at all.

Peter must have known he'd found my G-spot because he moved inside me so he could hit it over and over. I could feel myself cresting again, and I was helpless to do anything but ride the sensation.

As I began to climax, I could hear Peter coming closer to his climax as well. When it finally hit, I felt myself pressing down just as Peter cried out, "Oh God, yeah, yeah!"

I could feel Peter fill the condom, shudder behind me, and collapse across my back.

Peter pulled out, tossing the condom in a trash can next to the nightstand, then fell onto his back, exhausted.

I rolled, feeling a little self-conscious and not to mention a little sore, onto my side, and snuggled into Peter.

"Is this OK?" I asked.

"More than OK," he said. "I don't think I've ever had sex that good. Your body is so fucking responsive, Trevor." Then he kissed my head.

"Well, I don't have much experience, but it was pretty awesome for me, too!" I chuckled.

I'd never felt such a compulsion to snuggle as I did right then. The only other time I'd had anal sex, it was pretty bad. I'd gone out with an older guy I found on Grindr. I thought he'd be more experienced and able to help me do it the right way, but he'd only wanted to fuck. He didn't give a damn how it felt to me. Peter was his opposite. He'd been gentle and sweet and easygoing, giving me the lead. His sweet lovemaking clicked something inside me, and all I could feel was happiness as I pressed myself up against his body.

We both must have snoozed because I was surprised when I heard the beginning movements of Luka waking up next door. When I looked at the clock, it had been three hours since we'd put him down.

I slipped out of Peter's grip, quickly pulling my clothes on, and rushed into the bathroom to clean up before tending to my son.

When I came out of the bathroom, I was surprised to see Peter standing over Luka, talking sweetly to him. "You hold on little sport. Your papa will be right here to get you."

I came up behind him and kissed his back. "I'll take him," I said, and he stepped aside to let me.

Peter went into my bathroom, and I could hear the water running while I changed Luka's diaper. When he came back out, he asked, "Can I get something for you?"

"He needs a bottle. Can you hold him for a moment?"

Peter sat in the rocker as I handed him Luka before preparing the bottle. I'd heard my female friends say how seeing a man being sweet to a baby was like honey to a bee, but when I turned around and saw Peter holding my little one after passionately making love to me, I could literally feel my heart shift. As I stood there, watching the two of them, I realized I may actually be falling in love with this man. The thought both scared and thrilled me. Was it possible this could be happening to me? And when I had so much responsibility in my life?

Peter looked up at me and smiled with sleepy eyes. That's when my heart officially leaped over the edge. Fuckin' A... I was screwed.

Peter

I'd never thought much about having a little one. As a gay man, I just assumed it either wouldn't happen to me or if I met someone who wanted a baby, we'd eventually adopt. After having Trevor in my arms, then cradling Luka while gently swaying in the rocking chair, my heart ached.

The baby was so sweet, and I loved his little attitude, although I didn't really have to deal with it day in and day out like Trevor and Doris did. I thought it was a good indication of the little person's personality. Something about that made me want to protect him, nurture him, and make sure he got to grow up to be everything he could be.

I was thinking how odd these feelings were for a man who barely knew this baby or his father, when Trevor walked in. When I glanced up and saw the same blue eyes looking at me that I'd seen in his son, I felt my heart shift just a bit. The feeling caused me to smile.

Yes, I knew what love was. I'd been in love with Martin and had planned to spend my life with him, but my feelings for Trevor and Luka were different. They were paternal and nurturing for Luka, and hungry for his father. Although I'll never deny the feelings I'd had in the past, these new ones were pure in a way I hadn't felt before.

I smiled at Trevor, and his face blushed. Curious, I thought, but Luka squirmed in my grasp, and I realized he wasn't getting all the milk from the bottle.

"You are such a demanding little tike, aren't you?" I asked with a smile.

"You ain't seen nothing yet," Trevor replied. "Wait until he gets going on one of his tantrums. The boy can put any opera diva to shame!"

"Maybe you need to start him on voice lessons."

Trevor laughed. "Let's get him out of diapers first, then we'll talk about voice lessons."

After Luka finished his bottle, I lifted him to my shoulder and burped him while Trevor climbed into his bed across from us.

"Bet you never thought afterglow would include burping a baby, did you?"

I laughed. "Nope, you got me on that one."

Trevor's expression became serious. "Does it bother you?"

I didn't want to just blow him off, so I thought for a moment. "No, it certainly doesn't bother me, but it's a little disconcerting, though. I'd never considered being a parent until now, but having Luka in my arms after such an amazing experience with you makes me realize there's something magical about this co-parenting stuff."

Trevor sighed. "You know, I wouldn't blame you if you ran for the hills. I doubt I would have been a good sport if I'd been in your situation. Before Luka, I wasn't what you'd call good with kids. Luka sort of came at me out of the blue, as you know. But now, I couldn't... wouldn't want to imagine my life without him." Trevor looked at Luka as I held him, and I could see the tears glistening in his eyes. "Luka is everything to me." He seemed to catch himself then and chuckled self-consciously. "I'm a sap. I think a lot of the stuff blamed on hormones for new moms is really sleep deprivation." He chuckled again as he wiped his eyes. "Why don't you bring him over here and we can cuddle while he falls asleep."

I gladly complied, handing Luka to Trevor as I climbed into the big Victorian bed.

"This is a beauty," I said as I climbed up into the tall bed.

Trevor smiled. "My grandparents bought the house furnished, so all the beds came with it. The old lady they bought it from had no relatives, so almost all the furniture is original to the house. This was my mom's bed when she was growing up, and my grandpa thought it was only natural that when I moved in, I should get her room and this bed."

I turned toward him in surprise. "I knew the house was furnished to match the period, but I had no idea it was original. Have you ever had the furniture appraised?"

"Yep, my grandpa did all that. Here's some interesting trivia. Several of the pieces were 'too good' for a growing family, so my grandparents placed them on loan at a historical museum in Macon. In the nineties, when the boyhood home of one of the presidents was rebuilt, a couple pieces were placed there. So although my grandparents emigrated here, they had an investment in the history of Georgia and even the country."

I loved architecture and often that included furnishings. However, I wasn't as obsessed with those as I was the building themselves. "You must be enormously proud of that. Have you visited the museums?" I asked.

Trevor laughed out loud, which caused Luka to jump. "Oh, sorry, little man," he said while lifting him up to kiss his forehead.

"My grandpa marched Aunt Doris and me there every few months. I have both places memorized. He was proud of his 'investment in America,' as he called it."

I put my arm around Trevor and pulled him into my side. "That's really cool. I can't wait to go visit the museums with you."

"You want to do that?" he asked in shock.

"Um, the chance to get to hang out with two of my newest favorite men and be able to geek out over historical architecture? Yeah, count me in. In fact, can we leave now?"

Trevor laughed. "Let's wait a bit. If you still want to, maybe we can make it a fall trip."

I snuggled into him again. "That sounds awesome," I whispered into his hair.

We cuddled in the large comfortable bed, and at some point, I must have fallen asleep because when I finally woke up, the sun was up. Trevor was snuggled in beside me. The baby was in his crib, so Trevor must have woken up sometime before me and put him to bed. This shocked me because I was usually a light sleeper. It was unusual for me to sleep through anything.

I rolled over and spooned Trevor, and he nuzzled back into me. God, this felt good and right. Like I was meant, no, destined to be sleeping with this man in my arms.

I fell asleep like that and didn't wake again until I heard Luka stirring in the crib. Trevor snoozed next to me, so I extracted myself from him and got up to take care of the baby before he started crying. I'd changed a lot of my cousins' diapers, including the youngest, who was now only four, so I honestly didn't think anything of it.

I wondered if Luka ate this early in the morning and decided it was better to be wrong and feed him early than to wake Trevor up, so I heated the bottle as I rocked the sleepy little one in my arms. I was in the rocker and feeding him when I glanced up to see Trevor watching me.

"Morning sunshine," I said, smiling at him. "I was trying to be quiet so you could sleep."

Trevor just continued to watch me, making me feel nervous. "What, does he not eat this early?" I asked, afraid I'd upset him.

"I... um... I..." Trevor just stared at me after stammering. "No, no... he eats. I'm just shocked to see you doing it."

"Oh, sorry. My aunt used to leave her little ones with me. I used to make a killing off babysitting for her." I chuckled at the memory. "In our family, if a baby needs something, you don't wait for others to do it, you take care of it yourself. I apologize if I stepped over a line."

"No, you didn't. I'm just used to doing it all myself."

I smiled, careful not to say anything that would make the situation more awkward.

Trevor

It was strange when Peter fell asleep in my bed, and I just chalked it up to afterglow and exhaustion. I was even more shocked when in the middle of the night, he turned over and spooned me. The feeling was amazingly delicious.

The fact that Luka barely stirred in the night was a miracle in and of itself. I was used to a two-hour regimen of diaper changes, feeding and rocking, so the fact he slept for longer than five hours was truly miraculous.

I'd felt Peter stir and assumed he just went to the bathroom, so I let myself drift back to sleep. When he didn't come back to bed, I opened my eyes to see him sitting in the rocking chair next to Luka's crib, feeding him. Luka was almost back to sleep. Several emotions washed over me all at once. The first was fear that Luka wasn't well since he'd slept through the night, and second was relief that I'd had more than a couple hours sleep. The third was confusion. Why was a guy I'd just started seeing sitting in a rocker with my son who seemed extremely comfortable cuddled up in his arms?

I was so overcome with the emotions that when Peter noticed me, I wasn't able to talk. I didn't have a lot of experience with men, or women, for that matter, but it seemed strange to me that any man would be this comfortable around a baby. Was I overreacting? I'm overprotective, I know, but instead of setting off alarms, the sight of Peter and my son sent euphoric love bubbles straight to my heart.

"I'm calling your mom and asking her how she managed to turn you into a nanny," I said, making Peter laugh.

"You do that, and she'll be on the next plane to Atlanta to plan our wedding."

"Warning noted," I said, knowing that he probably wasn't exaggerating. Mrs. Reed wasn't a discrete woman. If she got word of our dating, she'd either hate me or order our wedding cake. I couldn't imagine what she'd be like if she thought a grandbaby would be included in the package.

I yawned and got up. "If you've got him, I think I'll take advantage of the moment and get a shower. You OK for a moment?"

"We're good," he said, looking down at Luka.

Was it weird I felt safe with him? I think I was struggling more with my lack of suspicion than the actual man. I'm suspicious by nature, especially after having parents from hell. I should be weirded out by all this, but instead, I felt... well, I felt safe. Really, I couldn't even blame sleep deprivation for this one. I'd had a full five hours, which was highly unusual since Luka had come into my life.

I climbed into the shower and immediately regretted that Peter wasn't going to join me. Another strange thought since I'd never shared a shower with another man before. I once read an Angelique Jurd romance novel, and the guys in the book showered together. While that was happening, the main character was getting fucked from behind. This was evidence I had no business reading romance novels while I was locked up in my metaphorical tower raising a newborn. It put crazy ideas in my head.

I finished showering and tried pushing away all the thoughts of what Peter's hands would've felt like as they lathered soap over me.

When I came out, both Peter and Luka were sound asleep in the rocker. *Now, that appeared much more natural,* I thought to myself. That whole "refreshed comfortable male" was too clean looking and felt a bit too much like magazine cover to be real. A tired guy asleep with a sleeping baby nuzzled in his arms, that felt real and natural in comparison.

And Peter did look natural with Luka in his arms. Luka, who seemed to wail when anyone he didn't know held him for more than a few minutes, seemed to possess a great deal of tolerance for the man as well. I wasn't going to question it for now. I was going to enjoy every damn minute of it.

I took Luka in my arms to burp him, assuming Peter had forgotten since he still held the empty bottle in his hands. When I picked Luka up, Peter's arms came around the little one protectively. "Shh, I got him," I replied.

Peter let go and opened one eye. "Sorry, I fell asleep, but I put my legs up on your bed so I wouldn't drop him."

"I wasn't worried," I said with a wink. "I'm going to burp him if you want to jump in the shower. Feel free."

Peter got up and did as I suggested, but I could tell he was still sleepy. Unfortunately, for me, sleeping time was all but over. I needed to keep Luka up for a few hours so he'd sleep this afternoon because I had a shit ton of work I needed to finish. If he slept now, he'd be awake this afternoon, and God help me, afternoon awake Luka was no fun to be around.

By the time Peter came out, I'd finished changing Luka into clean clothes and was just about to head downstairs. "Come down, and I'll make us some coffee," I said when I saw him.

"I have a better idea. You said mornings are Luka's favorite time. Why don't I take the morning off, and we can go to breakfast and have a walk around the park?"

I thought for a moment. "It'd be nice to get Luka out for a change. He could use the fresh air, and so could I for that matter. You sure you can take the time off?"

"Oh yeah, I have a lot of comp time built up after working all the extra hours on Richmond's project. Speaking of that, are y'all ready for the big party?"

"That's coming up in a couple weeks, right? Aunt Doris and Leonardo are constantly talking about it. If he isn't here or she isn't with him somewhere, they're texting one another like teenagers."

"They seem to really be getting along, huh?" Peter asked, and when I smiled at him, he chuckled. "Do you think they're getting serious?"

"Don't know and ain't asking," I replied. "The one thing I never, ever want to know about is my aunt's love life! Invite me to the wedding if it goes that far, otherwise, I like to pretend they're friends and that's that!"

Peter laughed out loud. "Yeah, I'm sure they are *real* good friends!" he said, then laughed again when he saw my frown.

"Yuck," was all I said as I walked out of the bedroom and down the stairs.

Peter

Luka seemed to enjoy the morning walk. We put him in his stroller and walked down toward a breakfast bistro that Trevor said the locals frequented. Had he not taken me there, I doubt I would've ever noticed it.

"How did you find this place?" I asked him.

"It's been here longer than I've been alive," he said. "My grandparents used to be friends with the owners, so we ate here a lot when I was growing up."

"Why don't they have signs?" I asked, taking in the nondescript building.

Trevor chuckled. "Do you think they could handle it if more people knew about it?"

I noticed the crowd then and saw that every table was occupied. "Is it like this every day?"

"No, sometimes it's busy," Trevor said, smiling.

"I see, so this is just by word of mouth."

"Yep, and we guard it as our neighborhood secret, so consider yourself sworn to secrecy."

"Got it," I said and smiled at him.

The food was a perfectly cooked Southern breakfast, with everything including biscuits and gravy made from scratch. "This is the first time in a while I've actually had homemade biscuits. Nowadays, it seems everything is pre-made."

Trevor sighed. "Ma Jackson is getting older. No one knows what'll happen when she retires, but until then, it'll be only food made from scratch served here."

"Restaurants like this one are becoming more and more rare as time goes on," I said with a sigh. "I'm glad you brought me here."

Trevor smiled and put his hand over mine. "Thanks for suggesting we take a morning out."

Everyone seemed to know Trevor, and Luka was a big hit. Trevor told me this was Luka's first time being here, and everyone kept coming by to make a fuss over the baby. I enjoyed watching Trevor in his element, smiling at a joke, or laughing about the gossip in the neighborhood. It shocked me how well the man seemed to fit in.

I wondered if maybe fifty years from now, he'd be one of the old men sitting in the crowded corner gossiping with one another. Would I want to be one of them?

We walked around the neighborhood and ended up at the park bench where I'd found Trevor on the morning he'd seemed not to have a friend in the world. We sat watching the ducks as Luka played with the mobile that hung from the handle of his stroller.

"It's beautiful here," I remarked.

"Yeah, it's one of my favorite places," Trevor answered. "But you already know that, huh?"

"I know it's a special place for you. Tell me about your grandpa. He sounded like an amazing man."

"He would've liked you. He was a short man with a huge personality. When he walked into a room, it lit up like a Christmas tree. He loved to laugh and was full of silly jokes. He had a Croatian accent that he tried to hide but failed. The story goes that when he was young, he'd tell anyone who'd listen that he wanted to be an American. At sixteen, he convinced his sweetheart, my grandmother, to run away with him to the US."

I smiled at him. "Did they end up in Atlanta first?"

"No, my grandmother's aunt lived in New York, so they lived with her at first. When my grandpa turned eighteen, he got his GED and enlisted in the Army. It was during Vietnam, but they didn't send him over. Instead, he worked in administration. He didn't tell us much about what he did, even when we pushed him, but from what we could figure out, it was pretty top secret. When the war ended, one of his buddies talked him and my grandma into coming to Atlanta. He worked for an Italian family that owned a large clothing store. Long story short, the couple he worked for had a son who had no interest in following in the family's footsteps, so when the owners retired in the eighties, they sold the store to my grandparents. It helped that Grandpa could speak Italian fluently. Later, they bought their own place. My mom called it the old haunted house. My grandpa's parents worked in construction in Croatia. He worked with his father when he wasn't in school, so he knew how to redo old homes. I sort of worry how we're going to keep it up now he's gone. I'm not as handy with a hammer as he was." Trevor chuckled.

"Maybe your aunt can handle it," I replied, only half-joking. I had no doubt Doris could do anything she put her mind to.

"Aunt Doris is more fashion and less construction, but yeah, she's not afraid of crawling on a three-story roof. Believe it or not, I've seen her and my grandpa working together on the gutters up there."

"Oh, I believe it."

"When my grandparents bought the house, the area was fairly run-down, and I think they planned to eventually move to a more affluent area, but by the mid-eighties, the neighborhood was improving. So, like with most things, my grandpa was in the right place at the right time."

Luka began fussing a little, so we decided to walk around the park as we talked.

"I love older homes, older architecture in general," I told Trevor. "Inman Park and Virginia Highland both intrigued me when I first arrived in Atlanta. I was lucky to find a firm located in the area, and I'm hoping I'll get to do more projects like I did for Richmond. Redesigning the older designs for modern uses inspires me."

"Do you prefer commercial or residential?" Trevor asked.

"I like them both," I admitted. "I'd love to work on some of the renovations of the Victorian homes here to modernize them while maintaining their historical charm, not unlike your grandparents did. I like that you moved the kitchen into the old library with the parlor opening onto it, that's both modern and convenient while preserving the music room in the front as a sitting room. There's always a way to respect the historical character of these homes while making them relevant for today."

Trevor was watching me as I spoke. "I like seeing your passion. You really did go into the right field, didn't you?" he asked.

"Yeah, I love it. How about you? Do you love being a PI?"

Trevor sighed. "I planned to go to law school. I always thought I'd like to be an attorney, but my plans got put on hold because of Luka. To be honest, I do think I love being a PI more than I'd like working in a stuffy law office. My clients are... colorful." He looked at me and smiled, and we both silently knew he was talking about my mother. "The job is flexible enough I can work during the day when Luka sleeps or at night when he doesn't."

"Do you think you'll stay with it?"

"Probably, I'm pretty sure my plans for law school are done. Once Luka is a little older, I'll take on more cases and see where it leads me. For now, though, I couldn't have asked for a better place to work."

When I dropped Trevor and Luka at home, I was feeling pretty euphoric, at least until I walked into the office and came upon my angry boss.

"Peter, I need to see you in my office," he said as he walked away. Assuming I needed to follow, I came up behind him.

When we got to his office, he closed the door behind me and asked me to sit in the chair across from him. I knew things were going to go badly when he started the conversation with, "I know things are different nowadays..."

I sighed and tried not to frown as the old man continued.

"Your life is your own, but as long as you work for me, you need to be more discrete."

"Mr. Franklin, I'm not sure what you're talking about."

"On my way into work this morning, as I drove through the park, I saw you and some man kissing, and were you pushing a stroller?" he asked.

I bit my tongue to keep myself from saying something I'd regret. When I remained silent, he sighed. "This is still the South, Peter," he continued. "We have several clients who'd have fired us if they saw that display. You represent the firm, and whether you like it or not, how you conduct yourself has a direct impact on us."

I continued to sit in silence, not wanting to be disrespectful and say something that would cause me to get fired. But I also didn't want to compromise my values and personal worth as a human being. I could tell my silence infuriated the man, but I was sure anything I said would infuriate him even more.

Finally, he stood up and crossed to the door. As he opened it, he said, "This is your warning, Peter. Keep your lifestyle to yourself, or I'll be forced to let you go."

I stood and left without looking at him but determined to keep my head high. This wasn't my first experience with bigotry, but it was the first time it threatened my livelihood. I'd keep my mouth shut, but I wouldn't hide my pride for who and what I am. No, I wouldn't give that up, not even for a job.

I checked over my schedule, made sure I could work from home, and let the secretary know I'd be out for the rest of the day. I know I was poking the bear, but if I stayed, I was sure by the end of the day I'd be fired anyway.

My anger grew as the day went on, and eventually, I decided to call my mother and vent. I knew she'd listen, console me, and hopefully offer some advice on how to proceed.

"It's unfair," she replied after I'd whined for about thirty minutes. "But you know there aren't any laws to protect you. You'll have to either sit quietly or quit."

I sighed. "I know, Mom. I'd quit, but this firm lets me explore my passion for retrofitting older designs with modern components. Well, more importantly, they're the only ones in town that have the clients who want that kind of work done."

"So, what're you going to do?" she asked.

"I don't know. For now, I'm going to spend less time in the office and more at home."

"Why don't you look for another firm?"

"I signed a non-compete. I can't work with anyone within a two-hundred-mile radius for two years."

"Oh." She sighed. "Well, you could come back home," she said hopefully.

I chuckled. "Because Texas is so much more open and accepting of homosexuality. Didn't they just pass a law that allowed doctors to refuse to treat gay people?"

"Yeah, well, that's true. But you know Austin's different from the rest of Texas."

"I know, Mom, but I've sort of met someone, and I'm not ready to move away just yet."

I knew I'd set myself up for hundreds of questions, but I needed to let her know I'd met someone anyway. I wasn't quite ready to let her know who yet because, well, she was who she was, and she'd done what she'd done. All that aside, I loved my mother and wanted her involved in my life.

Mom paused. "I'm working hard not to pry, Peter," she said, sounding timid. "But when you feel secure, I'd like to meet him, and I promise I'll be totally different than I was with Martin."

"Speaking of Martin," I said, deciding to shift the discussion and take advantage of my mother's changed attitude, "have you spoken to him again?"

"Yes, he and I have been corresponding but only through Facebook. He and Elian got married, you know. At first, I was really upset about Martin finding someone else and not being able to fix what I'd destroyed between you and him. But Elian really is good for him. I pray every night, Peter, that you can find someone like Martin has." She sighed a long sigh and paused, clearly not sure how to proceed.

"Mom, I forgive you. Martin is special, and I'm happy he found someone to love him, and I'm going to be OK. You can stop beating yourself up now."

She sighed again. "Until you have someone in your life, I'm not sure I can forgive myself. But I appreciate your forgiveness, son. Reconciling with Martin has really helped. It's strange to be communicating with him as much as I do, but I think he needed the reconciliation as much as I did. That whole experience was traumatic. The fact that I can remember it all so clearly, but can't reason why I acted so horribly... it's a lot to process, Peter. It's like someone else possessed me and lashed out toward him."

"Mom, in a way, that's what happened. I think that's why I couldn't understand what Martin was telling me back then. You may dislike someone, but you've never lashed out. It helps to know it was the tumor, but it took a long time for me to be able to forgive you."

I could tell she was crying but working to hide the tears.

"Mom, tell me this. If you could go back in time and change it, would you?"

"Of course, honey. I wish I'd known about the tumor earlier so I could've had the surgery or at least give some warning why I was acting the way I did, but I can't go back, as much as I want to... I can't."

"I know, Mom. But just knowing you'd do so if you could, that helps. Your remorse really helps me see that it wasn't intentional. I do have a question, though, since we're really talking about this now. Did you like him, really, or did your dislike for him influence you?"

Mom waited a moment before responding. "It's hard to say because I can't tell how much was the tumor and what was me. It gets confusing in my head, you know? I've thought about it a lot, though, and here's how I've reconciled it in my mind. If you'd brought Martin home, say, a year before you did and introduced me to him, I would've had some concerns. Most moms would, I think, because we want the best for our kids, but I think now that I know him, and he and I are getting along, I think I'd have grown to like him in the long run."

I thought for a moment about what she said. "So if you disliked someone I was dating now, or thought we weren't really a good paring, you could *learn* to like them?"

She didn't hesitate at all this time. "Yes, I would love them because you love them. That's all that's required now. I want you to find someone you love with all your soul, and I want them to love you the same way."

"What if they have a kid?" I asked, waiting to see if she put two and two together.

I wasn't disappointed. Her quick mind went straight to where I was headed. "You're dating Trevor?" she asked.

"You can't bug him, Mom. Promise me you won't."

"Of course not, honey. But just so we're clear, it's taken every ounce of willpower in me not to try to set you two up. He's such a good boy and insightful for his age."

I chuckled. "Well, thanks for not interfering. We are new, but I like him... I like him a lot, actually."

"Oh, honey, I'm so happy for you. And I promise, unless he reaches out to me, I'll keep my distance."

"Thanks, Mom. OK, I've got some work to do. Thanks for letting me vent, too. I needed it."

"Anytime, sweetheart," she replied. "Sometime in the future, I want to meet that baby, but only when you're ready."

I laughed out loud. "We'll see," I replied before we finished up our call.

***

After the confrontation with Mr. Franklin, work settled back into a normal routine. I spent much more time working from home, and no one seemed to notice or care.

I was given some freedom to help with the party, so I spent quite a bit more time with Doris and Trevor, making plans for the big reveal.

We'd gotten preliminary approval from the neighborhood and city for the store construction, and luckily, the neighborhood liked that we were building something reminiscent of the current architecture. The lot Richmond had purchased was one of the last derelict properties in the area.

Reporters began to swarm Trevor's property as news of the party got out. Unfortunately, I felt like I had to be discreet about my relationship with Trevor. I was concerned that if we were seen together, I could lose my job and be forced to move away from the man and his son, both of whom I was growing more fond of by the day.

When the invitations went out to the city's elite, which included the budding movie studio people, I knew I could no longer visit Trevor's home without being exposed. I didn't want to let Trevor know I was in jeopardy of losing my job, mainly because I was embarrassed I didn't have the backbone to stand up to my boss. The more I thought about the situation, the more I realized I didn't want to lose my ability to live in Atlanta. I liked the city, but I was beginning to love the man.

Luckily, Richmond kept me busy on-site, and we began clearing the debris and leveling the area for the new store, so when the press took pictures, there would be some noticeable progress. We'd already heard several positive comments from the city and neighbors about how nice it was to have the derelict lot cleared and cleaned up.

Richmond had an antique-looking fence installed around the property, which reinforced the idea that we were going to create something reminiscent of the character of the area. Politically, the man knew what he was up against. Several other infill programs had been proposed for this site and were immediately shut down by the neighborhood. I confessed to Richmond that if he'd wanted anything other than Victorian style, he'd probably never have gotten this far.

As things ramped up, neither Trevor nor I had time to spend together. I was surprised at how much I missed him and Luka. Was it possible to get this attached in such a short time? Apparently so. With Martin, our relationship had been a slow burn. With Trevor, I seemed to go from zero to one hundred within seconds of meeting him.

Luckily, we were able to talk on the phone every night. That just made me miss him more, though. Before it was all said and done, I was anxious for the damn party to be over so we could go back to the way we were before.

Trevor

For the most part, Aunt Doris took the lead at the party. I'd never seen her so inspired before, and I got caught up in the energy because of her.

I missed Peter more than I wanted to admit. I was almost sure I was getting overly attached because my predicament left me more vulnerable than I would've been otherwise.

Regardless, when we were days away from the big party, I was happy to see the end in sight.

I moved into a temporary living space on the top floor, and what was once a ballroom for the original owners. Apparently, the house was built so guests would go to the top of the house to party.

Luckily, my grandpa designed the space as a studio apartment. Although it was never used, it did give Luka and me a cool place to hide while our first floor was turned into a party venue for Leonardo's big reveal.

I was surprised at how much more I got done now that I worked up here. There were fewer distractions, and Luka even seemed to be more settled than when I'd worked from the first-floor music room. Once the party was over, I decided we'd spend our days up here working instead of downstairs.

Aunt Doris had the men Leonardo had hired to help prepare for the event, bring up a couple of comfortable couches she found at one of her consignment stores. Because we weren't in the main living area, both Aunt Doris and I didn't feel compelled to follow any architectural rules or period appropriateness with furnishings like we did in the rest of the house.

Peter visited us once before things got too hectic. And to my surprise, he didn't criticize us for being more casual up here. In fact, he even commented on how comfortable the space was with its vaulted ceiling and wide plank floors.

Of course, when Leonardo saw it, he had a hundred ideas about setting the space up for doing some photos for his online catalog. Luckily, Aunt Doris nixed it, saying, until the party was over, this was the family's personal space.

As the party drew closer, things seemed to swirl around us. I swear there were several days I didn't go down to the first floor at all. Leonardo hired us a nanny who sat with Luka when I had to run errands, and Aunt Doris wasn't available to babysit. I was reticent at first, but the older lady had years of experience working with infants and was probably better qualified to care for Luka than I was.

I didn't have to call on her often, but when I did, she was great, and Luka seemed to like her.

***

On the day of the party, I let the nanny take full responsibility for Luka. I was happy she'd sat with him some before that day because she had a handle on his peculiarities. I dashed up and down the stairs all day checking on him like the helicopter parent I was, but even during his tantrums, the nanny seemed to have him under control.

When Peter asked me to lunch, I readily agreed. I was hungry to get out of the house but also to spend time with him.

When we got to his car, Peter leaned over and kissed me, and I immediately melted in his arms. "Damn, Peter, I think I'm hungrier for you than food." I sighed.

"In that case, let's go to my place." And without waiting for my response, he put the car in reverse and took off toward his condo.

I laughed, then ran my hand over his crotch like I had the first time we'd headed to his condo for a quickie.

Peter moaned. "You don't play fair."

"Not when it's been this long," I replied, trying to sound like me rubbing his crotch was something I was entitled to do.

Peter chuckled, but this time he reached down and opened his pants and put my hand on his underwear-clad cock. It was my turn to lose control. My body ached to have Peter inside me. He didn't have to give any more of an invitation than he did. I bent over, pulled his cock out of his underwear, and took him in my mouth.

Peter moaned but maintained control as he drove. "Oh fuck, Trevor... your mouth feels so good," he uttered.

When we got to his condo, he zipped up, and we rushed to get inside.

We didn't make it to his bedroom this time. We stripped just inside the door. I went to my knees, taking his cock back into my mouth while Peter leaned up against the door.

"I want to taste you, Peter," I said, between sucking him. Then I pushed his cock deep into my throat and swallowed.

"Oh, fuck!" he cried.

He pulled me to my feet, and we quickly made our way back to his bedroom. Before we got to the bed, he asked, "Have you ever topped?"

I shook my head, but my cock jumped at where this appeared to be going.

"Do you want to try?"

My mouth went dry with anticipation, and I just nodded, unsure my voice would work.

Peter climbed onto the bed, reached over to the bedside table, and pulled out the lube, a condom, and a dildo. "Oh fuck, this is so fucking hot!" I replied mostly to myself, but Peter chuckled.

I watched as he lubed up the dildo and worked it into his very sexy hole.

I rubbed my own cock as I watched him prep himself for me. When Peter threw his head back and pushed the dildo all the way in, I crawled up beside him and kissed his chest, moving down to the yummy treasure trail, which flowed tantalizingly all the way down to his cock.

He continued fucking himself with the impressively sized dildo when I took his cock back into my mouth. Peter moaned loudly, and I matched his rhythm, sucking him as he fucked himself. I edged him over and over, which just seemed to make him thrust the dildo into his hole harder and harder.

Finally, I said, "Can I fuck you now?"

Peter nodded and smiled. "You'll need to use a whole lot of lube."

I blushed. "I don't have to if it's too much."

Peter laughed. "Oh, it's too much, but I'll be damned if I don't try. I want that monster inside me, Trevor!"

I leaned over and kissed him hard, moving to lie between his legs. I took the dildo from him and worked it around in his hole, stretching him as much as I could. When I pulled it out and positioned myself to replace it with my cock, I looked at it and smiled. "That's about the same size as me. It's sort of huge."

Peter laughed. "Yeah, they call it the doc. I've been using it to prep for this."

The thought of Peter using this giant dildo with me in mind made my heart stutter. "God, I dreamed of fucking you, Peter. But don't let me hurt you, OK?"

Peter smiled and ordered, "Stop talking and start fucking!"

I didn't need to be asked twice. After sliding the condom on and liberally applying lube, I lined my cock up and began head fucking him, slowly, not wanting to hurt him, but oh, how I wanted to grind his ass. I can't count the number of times I'd jacked off in the shower with Peter's ass in mind. I just never thought he'd let me try.

When Peter didn't seem to be in any pain, I pushed further in and watched for any indication he was uncomfortable. Luckily, the dildo seemed to have done its job because Peter was arching and beginning to push against me.

"Fuck, you're so tight, Peter. I could come just sitting here."

"Not yet," he said. "Not until you put that big cock all the way in."

"Can you handle it?" I asked, still unsure.

"Goddamn, stop asking and fuck me, Trevor!"

I laughed, and seeing he wasn't in any pain, I complied. I thrust my cock all the way in, and Peter moaned, then seemed to melt into the bed. I fucked his gorgeous ass, watching his face as it showed how much he was enjoying me.

"I want to fuck you doggie style like you did me," I said, anxious about his hesitation.

Peter pulled his legs up and spun around so fast, I laughed out loud.

"You are a horny fuck, aren't you?" I asked, feeling aggressive with the power fucking Peter had given me.

Peter nodded but didn't speak as I pressed my cock to his ass.

"You ready?" I asked.

Peter just nodded and pushed back against me, and I shoved in. "Oh, fuck! Yeah, yeah, Trevor... oh my God, that's just right."

I took that as permission to pound into him. Just like I'd dreamed of since the first time I touched him.

I fucked him, forcing his back into an arch. Then as the adrenaline kicked in, I shoved his face down into the pillow, pounding him with all my strength.

I had long ago given up hope any man would let me fuck them like this. I figured if I wanted to be the top, I'd have to be with a woman. And here I was, fucking Peter's tight ass just like I'd fantasized.

I didn't mind being a bottom. I loved it actually, but oh, the thrill of watching my cock rock in and out of this man was more than I could stand.

Peter moaned into the pillow as I took him, a monster inside me now in control. All I could do was drive my desire into him, wanting to claim him, wanting to make him mine and only mine.

Peter

Trevor's cock was bigger than the doc. I'd prepped myself craving that cock, craving him taking me just like this.

My mind was mush as he drove into me. Suddenly, he adjusted the angle and hit my prostate just right, and I blew all over the comforter.

When I squeezed down on him, he yelled out and released himself into the condom... the extra-large condom I'd had to purchase for him knowing none of mine would ever work on that large dick of his.

I couldn't move and fell over into my own wet spot. Trevor fell behind me, slipping his arm around me, holding me tight in a desperate grip.

Finally, he asked, "Are you OK?"

I nodded, still not able to catch my breath. I could tell he was nervous, so I turned and kissed him.

"You've ruined me."

His eyes registered what I said, and I saw panic cross his face.

I laughed. "Trevor, you have no idea what that was like. It was the best sex I've ever had. You are so tender, but your cock gives a really, really, *really* good punch. I needed that, something about you..." I couldn't figure out the words. "Sorry, my mind's still mush. You've ruined me for any other man. I'm going to follow you around for the rest of your life like a desperate puppy begging for more bone."

I laughed at my joke, and Trevor smiled.

"I never dreamed it'd be that good."

We were both still out of breath, so we stopped talking and just let ourselves bask in the glow of the most awesome sex I'd ever had... probably would ever have again unless it was with him. Trevor was everything I'd ever wanted plus a whole lot more.

Trevor

I didn't want to get up. I just wanted to lie next to this incredible man and maybe try round two, then maybe three and four, but responsibility forced me up. I got to my knees, kissed Peter squarely on the mouth, then walked into his shower.

When I turned the water on, I hollered out. "You coming?"

Peter yelled back, "I'm not sure I can move!"

I laughed. "Think I should call the paramedics?"

"Hell no, I'm not sharing that cock with anyone!" he replied, rushing into the bathroom to join me.

"I didn't say I was gonna share my cock. I think it's becoming pretty partial to you."

"Good," Peter replied. "Let's keep it that way."

Peter pushed me under the water and climbed in behind me. Using his taller frame to his advantage, he stood over me while lathering both our bodies with soap. When he had us both lathered up, he began humping me from behind. "I want to be fucked a lot, Trevor, but I still think that tight ass of yours needs it occasionally, too."

After rinsing me off, Peter knelt down and spread my cheeks. He let his tongue explore me. "Oh, fuck! Oh yeah, that's good." I gulped.

Peter chuckled but continued assaulting my hole with his glorious tongue.

I'd seen it in porn, but I'd never had it done to me before. "Shit, that's amazing!" I uttered and wasn't able to keep myself from pushing back onto his tongue as my cock grew hard with all the sensations. "Damn, Peter, I need you to fuck me. Do you have a condom?"

Peter pulled away without saying anything. I thought that was it, but just seconds later, he returned, opening a condom as he climbed back into the shower. "This will work," he said and smeared my hole with lube he'd brought with him. Peter slipped his finger inside and kissed me from behind as he prepped me.

"God, that feels so good!" I exclaimed. "But I'm ready, Peter... I want to give you the same pleasure you just gave me."

Peter growled and let his cock move up and down my lubed hole. When he pressed in, I tensed at the intrusion, but Peter pulled out and let his head prep me more. "You're so tight... you sure you want this after we just had sex?"

"Damn, I want this worse than I've wanted anything in a long time," I said.

Peter moved his cock over my hole again and again, then finally pushed back in. The intrusion caused me to tense again, but I held him against me. I forced myself to relax as the pain gave way to pleasure.

Peter stood still as I pushed myself back on him. I stroked my own cock as I fucked myself on his, letting myself get used to him, and enjoying the sensation of the warm spray pouring over us.

Finally, I nodded, and Peter moved again, slowly at first. Picking up on my movements, and seeing how much I wanted him to fuck me hard, he began pounding me. He thrust himself into me until I was pressed up against the tiles. He took me with the same passion I'd taken him with just a few minutes earlier.

I came without touching myself as my cock fucked up against the cool tiles. Peter pulled out of me and started stroking himself. Moving us out of the spray, I knelt down in front of him. He looked down at me and saw my open mouth. I was asking him to pour himself onto my face. The gesture seemed to energize him. He stroked into my mouth and, within minutes, spewed and coated my face and the floor tiles around us.

He shuddered as he emptied himself, then thrust his cock into my mouth, emptying himself the rest of the way.

I wasn't too surprised after our last kink fest when Peter leaned over and licked his spunk off my face.

"Fuck, that's so hot," I said as I enjoyed sharing his cum with him.

When Peter was done, he pulled me up, and we both rinsed off.

"I wonder when this isn't so new if we'll be able to do that back to back," I said.

Peter laughed. "You make me feel so fucking out of control. I don't think my ability to come with you will diminish any time soon," he said.

We climbed out of the shower, toweled each other off and, accepting our time was up, got dressed and headed out to Peter's car.

"You ready for this?" I asked him.

"The party?" he asked. "Yeah, it's not much on me. At this point, it's more the Doris and Richmond show... we just have to show up."

"I have to admit," I said as I climbed into the car. "I'm anxious to see all the different outfits. I'm not really into steampunk all that much, but it does seem to attract some interesting characters, you agree?"

"Oh yeah. Since I started this project, I've seen some really interesting stuff, and there's some strange kink associated with it, too. Although that's a little more underground than Richmond's stuff."

I chuckled. "Yeah, I ran up against some of that, too, while I was doing research. So I'd be prepared for tonight." I suddenly felt shy, looked over at Peter, and asked, "Are you into any of that?"

Peter laughed out loud. "Um, I haven't been, but if you wanted to try it out, I'm game."

"Really?" I asked, shocked that the straight-laced Peter Reed would even consider such a thing. "I'll have to think about it," I said, then shoved my shoulder into Peter's.

The mood evaporated the moment we pulled into my neighborhood. City officials had put up signs around the area about where parking was or wasn't allowed. Leonardo had made arrangements for parking at a local shopping center, and had a shuttle service set up, but it was strange to see my sleepy neighborhood covered with the sort of signs I was used to seeing at big events downtown.

Peter pulled his car into the backyard and parked next to the garage, where Aunt Doris had designated a space for him. There were several spots in the yard that could be used for parking, and only the most esteemed guests had them allocated. It shocked Peter that she'd set up one of those spaces for him. "You are the star of the show, Peter," she said with a smile and a wink upon greeting us, before turning away and getting back to last-minute party preparations.

Peter shrugged, realizing there was no room for argument and accepted the generosity of my aunt.

We walked into pure chaos. I pulled Peter up to the attic with me so I could check on Luka and get out of the insanity.

Luka was asleep, which was perfect for this time of day. Luckily, the insanity two floors down didn't seem to be disturbing his routine, which was exactly as I'd hoped.

The nanny looked up from her knitting as I came in and gave a report in a whisper. "He's done great. Only one meltdown, and that was shortly after you left, but once he got his diaper changed and his afternoon bottle, he was back to his cheerful self."

I knew she was exaggerating. Luka was never charming in the afternoon. At best, he was tolerable. I chuckled and said, "You're a good sport, Mrs. Graham."

She just smiled and went back to her knitting.

***

The party was insane. There were models walking around in bizarre steampunk costumes. There were TV screens around the room that featured models walking down runways, and interesting visuals of different steampunk items. And in the dining room, an automaton was working its magic.

I'd only ever seen them in magazines or on Facebook, so I was intrigued and fascinated by the odd engineering. Leonardo came up behind me and put his hand on my shoulder. "Hard to believe that it's working on a windup system, isn't it?" he asked.

"Yeah, it's hard to wrap your mind around a time when there were no computers, television, or electricity."

"That's what makes steampunk so fascinating, I think," he said but was immediately distracted by the mayor, who was being introduced to him by our local commissioner.

I smiled at them all as I disappeared to find Peter or Aunt Doris.

I wandered around the house, then into the part of the yard that was set apart for guests, when I heard raised voices. I saw my mom talking to Aunt Doris, and I immediately went toward them.

"Mom, why are you here?" I asked, not trying to hide my anger.

"You need to give that baby up!" she said, slurring her words.

"Mom, are you drunk?"

"Of course not," she replied, but the slur proved she had something in her system.

"Where's Dad?" I asked, concerned as to what kind of chaos he was planning. When she didn't respond, I said, "If you don't tell me where he is, I'm going to call the police. For God's sake, Mother, the mayor and half the city council are here!"

She blushed. "I don't know, he left me in the car. He told me not to get out, but I needed to tell you it isn't OK for a man of poor values and character to raise a child."

It took everything in me not to blow and luckily, my aunt stepped up before I said something that would make things worse. "You are the one with a bad character. You aren't welcome here, and we've told you that over and over. Leave now, or I'll be the one to call the police. And we'll have that restraining order you were warned about put in place tomorrow morning. Leave, Rita, *now!*"

My mother stuck her inebriated chin out and stalked toward the front of the house.

"Let's find my father before this gets ugly," I said.

Aunt Doris had already started walking toward the house. "I'm going to let the police chief know there's something going down. I saw him in the parlor earlier. You go check on Luka."

I felt the bottom of my world drop out. Luka, I'd forgotten about Luka. I ran into the house, dodging guests, and taking the stairs three at a time. My world stopped when I saw the nanny slumped over in her chair. "Where's Luka?" I cried, but she didn't respond. I rushed to his crib, then searched the attic. He was nowhere to be seen.

I ran back down the stairs. I could feel the world spinning around me. Darkness threatened to creep into my vision, but I couldn't let myself fall apart... I had to find Luka. I had to stop my father and mother from whatever they had planned.

When I saw Aunt Doris from the landing, her face paled. She turned the man who she was talking to around, and when he saw me, he rushed over. "I'm Police Chief Adams. What's wrong?" he asked in a gruff voice.

"Luka's gone!" I said, and I fell to the landing, unable to keep myself upright any longer. "My baby's gone. I didn't keep him safe."

I don't remember much of what happened next, but everything happened in slow motion. Eventually, I felt Peter by my side, and I was being pulled up toward the second floor.

Later, I found out that the party had been stopped, and everyone searched while an Amber Alert had been sent out for Luka.

The police chief had questioned me immediately after the nanny had been rushed to the hospital. Apparently, my father—we all assumed it was my father—had drugged her. I thought to myself, *thank God she isn't dead.* But then I burst into tears. Would he harm Luka? Yes, he was capable of anything.

When I was questioned, I told the detective my father was violent, that he'd broken my arm as a child, and all the other things he'd done to abuse me when I'd lived with him.

The police assured me they were doing everything possible. But I knew my father. I knew what he was capable of, and I knew they wouldn't find him. The man was conniving. He wouldn't have put himself in jeopardy, wouldn't have jeopardized his standing in the community, unless he felt like he could wriggle out of this somehow. I doubted I'd ever see my son again.

Peter

Days slowly clicked by, and I stayed with Trevor as much as I could, but he'd grown cold toward me. I could tell he was pushing me away... pushing everyone away.

"You can't blame yourself, Trevor," I finally said after a long session of him staring out the window.

I must have hit a nerve because he turned his gaze toward me and said, "Then who do we blame, Peter? My son was kidnapped by *my* parents, from *my* house, because of a stupid party. It should've been me there with him, not a damned nanny, not someone who didn't know what kind of man my father is. If I'm not to blame, Peter, then who is?"

I knew he was spewing anger at me, I knew the accusation was directed at me, and it wasn't like I hadn't already blamed myself.

"You can hate me, Trevor, but Luka needs you. He needs you to be strong."

Trevor put his head in his hands and wept. "There's nothing I can do for him now, is there?"

Doris came into the room. The bags under her eyes were deep. She hadn't slept much either, and she looked utterly exhausted.

"Trevor, we need to talk," she said.

When Trevor didn't acknowledge her, she came and sat on the bed next to me. "Trevor, the detective thinks you should do an interview with one of the reporters he trusts and make a public plea to your parents to bring Luka back safely. They think it's possible your parents might regret what they've done and may want to bring him back or turn him in to someone who can care for him."

Trevor turned toward his aunt, but his face was devoid of emotion. "We both know my father couldn't give two fucks what I think, and if he took Luka, he's either killed him or stashed him with someone else. Anything to hurt me, that's what this is. Getting even with me for leaving when I was ten."

Tears dripped out of one of Doris's eyes, but she remained stoic. "Honey, you need to appeal to your mother. She must have been drugged when we saw her that night. If we appeal to her, she may do the right thing."

Trevor's eyes continued to stare blankly at Doris. "You know she won't go against my dad. It doesn't matter what he does."

Doris stood and went to Trevor, kissing his forehead. "Think about it. Even if there's a small chance it'll help, it'd be worth it, don't you think?"

When Trevor didn't respond, she left the room and us.

"You should go, too, Peter," he said, staring me in the eye. "I no longer want you here."

I sighed. "You can't be alone right now. But if you want me to go, I will."

I could tell by the way Trevor was acting, he was thinking bad thoughts. I'd be damned if I'd let him sit there alone, but I could also tell my presence in the room with him was making things worse.

I walked out of the room and saw Doris about to descend the stairs. "Doris, wait," I called. "I don't want Trevor to be alone, I don't like the state of mind he's in. Can you sit with him while I call in a few favors? We need to give him twenty-four-hour surveillance. If he thinks his dad has harmed Luka, he's a danger to himself."

"I agree," Doris replied. "I'll go back in and sit with him, but please don't give up on him, Peter. He's angry at the world, not you, honey."

"I know, I'm here for the long haul."

I went out to my car and had a good cry. I did blame myself for distracting Trevor. He knew his parents were trouble, but I hadn't really acknowledged how much trouble they could be.

I called my mom and gave her an update on how things were going. She surprised me by saying she'd already bought a plane ticket and was headed my way. "We'll be there for that boy, no matter what."

I wasn't sure if I was happy Mom was coming, or upset. Matilda was a whole lot, but right now, I really needed someone in my court.

I also called Joshua and asked if he could come and help. "We need all the help we can get, and you and Trevor got along well when we hung out."

Of course, he hesitated. "I... I don't know him very well, Peter. Are you sure that wouldn't be weird?"

"It'll be weird, but he needs it. Right now, I don't care what's weird if it'll help him stay safe."

"Ok, I'll come by later tonight after work," he said.

My mother arrived the next morning and took a taxi to my condo, then came straight over to Trevor's. She walked in, and after greeting Doris, immediately got to work helping to clean up from the party. I'd never been so happy to see her or thankful for her Southern mom way of quietly getting things done.

Trevor seemed to do well with Joshua. When he was there, they seemed to be in a bubble and talked about stuff that didn't have anything to do with Luka or the mess we were currently in.

Mom usually sat in the rocking chair in his room while he slept. Trevor seemed to do the best with her as she poured "momness" all over him, assuring him that Luka was safe. "Grandparents can't resist the charms of a grandbaby, no matter how awful the grandparents are... it's something God does to us," she assured him. "It's like a grandbaby curse or something."

I was outside the room when I heard her tell him that and heard his chuckle. I thanked the good Lord in Heaven that Matilda was the hard-ass, loving momma she was.

Trevor

I blamed myself. Every ounce of self-hatred I'd ever felt after my father broke my arm washed over me again and again but one hundred times worse. As much as I didn't want to, I also blamed Peter. If I'd never met him, I'd still have Luka in my arms. It wasn't his fault, not really, but that didn't keep me from feeling these feelings anyway.

Mrs. Reed, she was the one who began pulling me back. I was shocked when she came up that day, carrying a tray with apple juice and chicken soup. "You need to eat, honey," she said to me like she'd been there all this time, not even going through the usual greetings.

"Where... when... Matilda?" I stammered, forgetting to use her formal name. "When did you get here?"

"Well, honey, I've been here a couple days," she said. "I came when I heard about all this. I figured my Peter needed his mom and now I can tell you need one, too. So eat up, OK? I'm baking a pie, and I'll bring you a piece when it's done."

"I... I..." I stammered, not knowing what to say. Finally, I went with the basics. "I'm not really hungry."

"Nonsense, you haven't eaten in the two days I've been here, and I'd be remiss as a mother if I let you get yourself sick. That baby is going to need you to be one hundred percent when he comes home, so stop sulking and eat." She came over to me, then and kissed me on the forehead like my aunt always did.

The tears threatened to fall again, but Matilda didn't pay them much heed. She pointed at the tray and said, "Eat all that, and when you're done, I want you to get a shower... child, you know I love ya, but you smell."

With that, she sauntered out of my room.

Aunt Doris, Peter, and his friend Joshua had all been in and out of my room, and nothing had made me feel better, but there was something about Matilda Reed that brought light into my darkness. Maybe it was that she wasn't pitying me... maybe it's because, as a mom, she knew how much I had to lose.

I did as she asked and attempted to eat the food. It sat sour in my stomach, but I forced myself to swallow down the soup. She was right, if, and that was a huge if, I got Luka back, I needed to have all my strength. I couldn't be a blubbering idiot. He had to be so scared.

The thought almost sent me back down the rabbit hole, so I stilled my mind, stripped, and got in the shower.

Numbness had long ago replaced the tears. But I allowed myself to cry again as I stood under the spray. Thoughts of Peter holding me that horrible day brought both guilt and comfort. I'd been cruel to Peter, but even now, I couldn't hold back my anger. Yet no matter how hateful I was to him, or what I said, he always seemed to be there.

When the water ran cold, I'd decided the days of self-wallowing were over. My father had taken my son, that we were sure of. But where he was taken, the cops hadn't been able to say, and I had been no help... well, Matilda's strength must have found its way inside me because I'd be damned if that was going to continue. This person, this weak, pitiful person, was exactly what my father expected, and for the past week, I'd given it to him just as predicted.

When I came out of the shower, I was a changed man. I dressed and went downstairs, where Joshua, Aunt Doris, and Peter were sitting. "It's time to change things up," I announced as Matilda came into the room.

"It's time we give that son of a bitch some action. Aunt Doris, if that reporter still wants to interview me, set it up. Also, if the detective will come back over, I have some ideas where they might be hiding Luka."

I looked over at Matilda and almost lost my resolve. "Matilda, I need you to keep me from turning back into a noodle. You're right, Luka needs me, and the days of self-pity are over."

She winked at me, then wiped a tear from her cheek. "Did you eat that soup?" she asked, and I chuckled.

"Yes, ma'am," I replied.

"Good, I'll go fix us all some pie," she said and disappeared back into the kitchen.

Peter

The next day, the detective and reporter came to interview Trevor and Doris. The reporter did a great job pulling the heartstrings, and both Doris and Trevor broke down several times as they begged Trevor's parents to bring the baby back home.

When the interview was over, Trevor thanked them and disappeared back up to his room. I followed him. "You OK?" I asked.

"I'm exhausted," he replied. "I know you've been worried about me, Peter, and I can't thank you enough for bringing Joshua and Matilda in. But right now, I need to sleep off that interview. It was a lot harder than I thought it would be."

I came over and sat next to him. "Can I hold you while you sleep?"

Trevor's expression was solemn. "I want that..." Then he lowered his gaze. "Sometimes I hate you, Peter, not as much as I hate myself, but I can't help it... I blame you for keeping me from him, for allowing my dad the opportunity to steal him."

I just sat and listened to Trevor as he admitted what I already knew.

"I'm sorry, Trevor. I blame myself, too, and when Luka is back safe and sound, you can tell me to take a flying leap, and I'll leave and never bother you again. But until then, I'm not going to desert you, and I'm not going to desert Luka either. So for now, you're stuck with me. Got it?"

Trevor looked at me, then laid down and pushed his back up against my leg. I kicked my shoes off and laid down next to him, spooning him from behind.

We laid like that for hours, with me holding him and eventually hearing his heavy breathing, telling me he'd finally fallen asleep.

The shadows outside grew longer, and I finally decided to pull myself away so I could watch the evening news and see how the interview turned out.

Luckily, Trevor just rolled over as I pulled away. I knew he hadn't slept hardly at all since Luka had been taken, so any sleep he could get was worth more than anything we could do.

I joined Doris and my mom in the music room, where they kept the TV. The news had just started. "Is he still sleeping?" my mother asked.

"Yeah, thank goodness," I replied.

Mom nodded at me and scooted over so I could sit next to her. The news started with them saying there were no new leads in the Luka Kovachich case, but they were leading with an interview with the family.

The reporter introduced the segment, reminding the audience that Luka had allegedly been kidnapped by his grandparents during Leonardo Richmond's steampunk fashion store coming-out party. Both their pictures were put on the screen.

They showed a quick clip of Richmond being interviewed, and the audience could easily see how upset he was. When asked if he was going to continue with construction, he simply said, "No, we are waiting to hear that little Luka is OK before we move the project along."

I could only imagine how angry my boss was. I hadn't called in again since I'd told the secretary I was going to take time off until I wasn't needed by the family any longer.

The reporter also announced they'd tried to reach the baby's mother, but she and her family had seemed to disappear as well. That was news to me, and I wondered why the detective hadn't told us.

That information settled into the back of my mind, though, as they introduced the interview with the victim's family.

The camera showed Trevor and Doris sitting together on the front porch and it was clear both were distraught. It was also clear that they loved the baby, and when Trevor said, "Every moment he's without his family, the trauma increases. He needs to come home. Mom, Dad, please bring him home," tears streamed down his face as he spoke straight to the camera.

When Doris chimed in, she asked that anyone who saw them or the baby, to please report it immediately to the police.

The reporter stood outside the house then, and before she spoke, the camera focused on me as I turned to follow the family into the house. I stood to the side more as moral support for Trevor than anything else.

When the camera settled on the reporter again, she said the baby's grandparents disagreed with Trevor's lifestyle, but no matter how much they might disapprove, the baby needed to be returned safe and sound.

The intent was to make a plea to the family to do the right thing, but it had come across as both homophobic and mean spirited. I was livid, not only that they'd said something that indicated it was somehow Trevor's fault, but also because they filmed me without my permission.

If anything, that stunt helped his parents justify their actions.

I was so angry I could've punched something, and both Doris and Mom looked at me.

Neither said anything as I stood and walked to the front door.

By the time I got outside, my phone was ringing. The caller ID read Edmond Franklin. I knew I shouldn't answer, but dammit, at that moment, I couldn't help it. I was so mad that someone would use this to push an agenda.

When I answered, the ass didn't even say hello. Instead, he said, "I warned you, Peter. Now you are on the evening news? I'll have your desk cleared tomorrow, and you can come collect your things from the receptionist."

He hung up before I could say anything, which made things worse. At least I could've had some closure by telling the bigot to go to hell.

I sat on the front porch swing for a long time, digesting all that had happened. The main decision I came to was that no matter what, I didn't want Trevor to see that footage. Not until his son was home... then we'd deal with the homophobia. Luka was, first and foremost, our priority.

Trevor

I woke up with a start. I'd forgotten to check on Luka, but when I turned to get out of bed and saw the empty crib, I almost died then and there. How could I have forgotten? Then I remembered Peter had cuddled me until I'd fallen asleep.

I got up and ran my hand over the empty crib, willing that wherever he was, Luka was safe and happy.

It was still the wee hours of morning, so I went quietly down the stairs and into the kitchen to fix myself a cup of coffee.

I was surprised to see Peter there, sitting at the counter looking at his laptop.

"Why are you up so early?" I asked, startling him.

He closed his laptop and peered at me through haggard eyes.

"Damn, you look worse than I do." I chuckled.

Peter smiled back, but the expression didn't make it to his eyes.

I immediately got nervous. "What? Have they found Luka?" I asked, panic taking over.

"No, no. I just had a run-in with my bigot of a boss. I'm trying to figure out what to do about it."

"A run-in, like how bad?" I asked.

He shrugged. "Well, about as bad as it gets, I'm afraid."

"Oh shit, he fired you?" I asked.

Peter shrugged again.

"Why? Was it because of this?"

"It's because I'm gay. It has nothing to do with you."

I sighed. "Yeah, sometimes it's easy to forget we're still in the South. What are you going to do?" I asked.

"I'm fine. I have plenty of savings, and he'll have to give me severance. I've already had my attorney go over the contract I signed when I went to work there. I'll call them later and see what advice they give. Anyway, you have plenty to think about besides my crazy mixed up shit."

"It's all the same shit. Your bigot boss, my bigot parents." I sat down next to Peter and put my head on his shoulder. "Thanks for being here for me, Peter."

"Always," he whispered as he kissed the top of my head. "Want some ice cream? I went out last night and got the good stuff. Ben and Jerry's Chubby Hubby!"

I genuinely laughed for the first time since I'd lost Luka. "You really bought Chubby Hubby?"

"Yep, my favorite!"

"Then, by all means, scoop me up some. I was going to make coffee."

"Yeah, that's a good idea, too. I doubt I'll be sleeping anytime soon, anyway. I'm too damned mad."

I kissed him on the cheek, not wanting to get my morning breath on him, then went to the coffee maker, set it up, and turned it on.

I came back and snuggled back into his shoulder. "This is really uncomfortable. Let's go to the living room and watch some TV or something. I could use the distraction, and from the look of you, you could too."

"You go ahead," he replied. "I'll just get us some ice cream."

I turned the TV on, and the news was playing. "Man found on the side of the road just outside Montgomery's city limits by a cyclist. As yet, the man hasn't been identified..."

Peter came in and walked over, took the remote, and said, "The last thing we need is other people's bad news."

I nodded in agreement as he changed the channel. When he came across an old *I Love Lucy* episode, he smiled. "You up for this?"

I chuckled. "My grandpa actually owned all these DVDs. I know them all by heart."

Peter sat next to me, and we watched as Lucy and Ethel pulled some ridiculous plot out of their ass and began implementing it. The episode was the one where Lucy ended up covered in grape juice from a vineyard.

We'd finished the ice cream and Peter was about to get us both another cup of coffee when there was a knock at the door. He glanced at me, then at his watch. "Who could it be at this hour?" he asked.

I just shook my head. "No one I know."

Peter found his phone, dialed nine-one-one, and said, "Push send if I tell you to, OK?"

I nodded.

Peter went into the entry hall and yelled back, "Trevor, it's the police!"

I rushed around him and pulled the door open. "Luka, did you find Luka?" I asked.

The cop just shook his head. "No, I'm afraid not. May we come in?"

"Of course," I said while Peter opened the door wider.

When the two officers were in the main room, one said to me, "We need to know your whereabouts last night."

"I've only been here for the past week," I answered, confused by the question. "Why?"

The officer turned toward Peter. "Can you verify that he's telling the truth?" he asked.

"Yes, my mom and his aunt Doris can as well."

The officer sighed. "If you could get your aunt, I have news I need to share with your whole family. The detective on your case is on his way as well."

My stomach roiled, and Peter said, "Want me to get her?"

"No, I'll do it. I need to let my stomach settle a bit anyway."

I woke Aunt Doris and brought her downstairs. By the time we were back in the room, the detective had arrived and took over from the officers.

"I'm afraid I have some bad news, but not about Luka," he quickly reassured me. He looked at me for a moment. "I'm afraid we found your father's body this morning in Alabama. He was found outside Montgomery."

The shock took a moment to register. "My dad is dead? Where's my mother? Luka?"

He shook his head. "We aren't sure. We assume they're nearby, but we aren't sure where. At least not yet."

Peter stepped up. "The news said last night that Luka's mother and her parents were also missing. Do you think this has to do with them?"

The detective sighed. "I'm sorry you heard it in that way. The reporter took some liberties with information she overheard from one of our other officers. Honestly, she's never done this kind of thing before, or we'd never have trusted her on this case."

Peter nodded, his face ashen.

"So, Lisa is missing?" I asked.

"Yes, we tried to reach her right after Luka's disappearance, but the house was empty. We tried to reach them again, but no one ever came back. So we've had surveillance on their house."

"I'm confused, you think Lisa is involved in Luka's kidnapping? Why? She's avoided my phone calls since she gave Luka to me. I've tried texting or calling her at least once a week. Hell, I've even tried going to her house, but no one answered my knock even though I could tell they were home. If she wanted Luka, she could've come here anytime. This doesn't make sense."

The detective sighed. "We're looking into it. The neighbors have told us they haven't been home since before Luka disappeared. It's possible they are involved somehow. It's just too soon to tell."

"Do I need to identify my father?" I asked.

"No, we had enough information on him to do that without you. For now, we just need you to sit tight, and if you hear anything from your family or Lisa, please let us know as soon as possible. It's possible this has to do with the interview. We think it's a good possibility they'll try to talk to you sometime today. I'm posting one of the officers with you in case they do. Time is of the essence here."

The detective had said that over and over since we first met him. But, I agreed.

When he left, Matilda came into the room. "I heard everything. Why don't you get the officer to come in? I'd prefer he be in here with us than out there. That way, if anyone calls, he'll be right here to help."

I nodded, but Peter beat me to the door. He invited the officer in and explained we'd prefer he was inside if we needed him.

He said that was fine, and we set him up in the parlor, so he had access to all of us, including the front door, if anything happened.

***

Peter and Matilda stayed in the parlor with the officer while Aunt Doris and I set up camp in the music room. Aunt Doris paced the room while I sat on the settee we almost never used because it was so uncomfortable. There were so many things we needed to say, but neither of us seemed to be able to say them.

Finally, Aunt Doris took the lead. "We should've prosecuted him back when he broke your arm. We just thought we were doing the right thing. I'm so sorry, Trevor."

"I'm so sick of the word 'sorry,'" I replied. "No offense, Aunt Doris, but the only people who should be apologizing are my parents. The rest of us are just reacting to their behavior."

She stared at me for a moment, then shook her head. "When did you get so grown up?"

"Having a little one depending on you will do that to you," I said with a sigh. "I just want him back safe and sound."

"Wanna talk about your dad?"

"There's nothing to talk about. A bad man died. It sucks because I should probably feel some remorse, but all I feel is relief and fear that he didn't die soon enough to save my Luka." I tried to hold back the tears. "Aunt Doris, my feelings for my father were long ago destroyed by his hate and aggression but my little Luka..." That's when the tears began to flow. "He is everything to me. Losing him means I lose myself."

"I know, honey, I know." Aunt Doris came over and pulled me into a tight hug. "I believe he's OK. I think maybe Lisa's family has him and they're hiding out somewhere."

I looked up at her. "So how did Dad die? Who would've shot him?"

"The most obvious person would be your mom."

"No," I replied. "That isn't her way. She'd have turned the gun on herself before she'd have shot him. Remember, she threw everything away, her family, her part of the shop... me. She threw all that away for him."

Aunt Doris nodded. "I thought the same thing but, honey, we never know what someone will do when a baby is involved. None of this is helpful. Guessing only makes it worse, I think. Unless it helps find Luka, let's try to focus on the positive."

"The positive being that one less hateful, abusive man is on the planet?"

Aunt Doris didn't reply. Instead, she hugged me tight again. "The positive is that Luka is still out there, and we're just a little closer to finding him."

The day stretched on and progressed slowly as the four of us did everything in our power to keep busy as we waited for answers. Around five, Joshua came over with two large pizzas proclaiming that pizza had a way of curing all ills. Of course, he had no idea what had happened since we last saw him but I hugged him anyway. "Thanks, Joshua, I can't tell you how much it means that you've been here for us."

Joshua blushed. The man really was adorable. I couldn't see Peter and him together, they seemed more like siblings to me than lovers, but I could see why any man would be attracted to him.

We filled him in on the loss of my father, and he rested his hand over mine. "I have a controlling father, one who has the emotional capacity of a Greek statue. I understand some of your pain..." Then he side hugged me and got up to head into the kitchen.

When he came back, he had several wine glasses and a bottle, which he opened. "It looks to me like we all need a little wine." As he poured, I couldn't help but notice he was struggling with his own demons. Peter had told me a little about his father. Not for the first time in my life, I thanked God in Heaven for my grandfather and Aunt Doris.

If it hadn't been for them, my life story would've been quite different.

The detective, along with another officer I didn't recognize, came to the house a couple hours after Joshua and asked a lot of questions about my father and Lisa's family.

Unfortunately, I was little help. I could only tell them what I knew from my childhood before I'd turned ten. After that, I was no longer around Lisa's family. If we saw each other, it was at school, and when we both became teenagers, we'd meet in town, somewhere we could take a bus.

"Lisa is the responsible one of the two of us. She's smart, funny, strong-willed... but her family was controlling, more than my parents, really. She grew up a very conservative Catholic. In fact, they were probably more conservative than the Southern Baptists. Before we were born, they joined some spin-off of the church that has teetered in and out of

Atlanta's Catholic Archdiocese. I don't know what Lisa's father did, but he somehow worked for that church."

"He was a deacon," the officer told us.

"So, do you think he's involved or was he somehow kidnapped? I don't understand."

"We were hoping you'd be able to shed some light on that yourself," the man said with a sigh. "Did you and Lisa have contact after the baby was born?"

I'd already answered that question multiple times. Still, I figured they were asking the same questions over and over to try to find anything I might have left out.

I explained again how I didn't know Lisa was pregnant and that right after New Year's, she met me at a diner and gave the baby to me. The detective admitted they'd already talked to the owner of the diner, and she'd confirmed my story.

Peter and Joshua were sitting in the room with us, and they both admitted they were at the diner that day, too... but that was before we knew each other.

I could tell the detective thought that was strange. Hell, I thought it was strange, but I knew neither of them was involved with the kidnapping. Why would they be?

I shared that Lisa told me she was concerned that her family would disown her if she kept Luka. Therefore, she'd completely pushed me and the baby out of her life.

I knew I hadn't given them any useful information. Nothing to help find my son, and I felt both hopeless and gutted to think he was out there with no one to protect him.

"Tell me this," I asked the detective. "Do you have any leads that point to Lisa or her family? Is it possible they were working with my parents?"

"Do you think Lisa would kidnap the baby?" he asked again.

"It's like I've told you before, Lisa could've had access to the baby anytime she wanted. I've been trying to reach her for months. Hell, I'm a private investigator, or have been for the past few months. I know she lived with her parents, and I know she didn't go out much. I even planned to try to catch her, but besides going to church with her parents, I don't think she's been out."

The detective looked at me. "So, Lisa hasn't been going out since she gave you the baby?"

"I mean, I didn't follow her every movement, but yes, when I was trying to find a time to confront her without her parents, all my evidence showed she didn't go anywhere other than her home or church."

The detective thought for a moment. "Was Lisa someone who tended to stay at home before the baby?"

I chuckled. "Absolutely not, her parents drove her crazy, and she hated the church they went to. I just assumed after Luka was born, she needed their connection. I can't imagine she isn't distressed about leaving him."

The other officer asked, "Trevor, do you think Lisa's father is capable of murder?"

I was shocked. I don't know why I never thought of Lisa's father as a suspect in my father's death. I shook my head. "I-I didn't know him very well," I admitted. "I only went over there a couple times, and that was to pick Lisa up, but I didn't really meet him. He was always gone."

"Was Lisa afraid of him?" he asked.

I thought for a long moment. "No, I wouldn't say afraid. Wary of him, maybe. She never let any of us come over to visit, they were a pretty closed off family. Lisa and I would tease each other as we grew older about who had the worst parents and she'd tell me things he'd done, but it was always things like making her go to church when she didn't want to, or that she had to wear clothes that looked like she was from the eighteen eighties. She never mentioned violence... except once she told me he was a 'spare the rod' kind of parent."

The officer sighed.

"I wish I could be more help, but Lisa and I were only a twosome. We didn't really have friends outside our friendship. Even in high school, it was just the two of us."

"What about at university? Did you have separate friends there?" he asked.

"Yes, Lisa had a roommate. Her name was Julia, I think. I didn't hang out with her much. She also pledged at a sorority but dropped out before it got to rush week. She said if she wanted her every action to be controlled, she'd move back home."

The officer wrote down what I said, and I hoped it at least gave them a couple more leads.

Before they left, the detective said, "We're going to make Lisa and her family 'persons of interest' in the case. That means their names will be given to the public as people to report if they are seen. If you think of anyone or anything else that might help us find them, please let us know."

Again, I felt hopeless and empty. Lisa and I had been as close as anyone could be over the years, but I felt like I didn't really know her at all. "I wish I could be more help. I'll try to remember who else I know that might know Lisa more than I do... but I suspect her father's church would be your best connection to him. They spent most of their time there."

Both men nodded and stood to leave. "We'll let you know as soon as any information comes in. Meanwhile, please keep us informed if anyone calls."

They left along with the officer who'd spent the day with us. I was almost disappointed to see the officer leave because as long as he was here, there was some hope that something would happen, we'd get a break in Luka's case.

I went to bed, knowing I'd just toss and turn, but I'd rather be next to Luka's crib than anywhere else. I'd come to think of the crib as him, and while there, it almost felt like he was home, although I knew it was just a delusion. It made me feel marginally better.

I was lying face-up, staring at the ceiling, when my phone pinged. I thought about ignoring it, thinking it was someone who was just giving comfort or support, but since I wasn't asleep, I picked it up and looked at it.

It was from a number I didn't recognize. The message read:

Oberton Road, Alabama, Red Barn

It didn't register at first what it meant or that it was important. I just thought someone had mistakenly sent me a text. But Alabama was what alerted me. My dad was killed in Alabama.

I immediately jumped up and ran downstairs to get the detective's number. He'd given us his card and told us to call if anything happened.

When he answered, I could tell he'd been asleep. "I'm sorry to wake you, detective, but I just got an odd text of an address. Oberton Road, Alabama, Red Barn. Do you think that could be a clue?"

The inspector quickly said yes and asked me to forward the message to the number I'd just called.

I sat in the parlor alone, choosing not to wake the rest of the house until I knew if the information was useful or not.

Around two in the morning, I got a call from a blocked number. I answered it immediately. "Hello?"

"Trevor Kovachich, come to the address I'm texting you. Come alone, or the baby will die. Do you understand?"

I nodded and realized the caller couldn't hear me. "Yes. Yes, I'm coming."

"Alone," the caller repeated.

"Alone," I agreed.

When I hung up, I immediately called the detective again and told him what had just happened. I'd seen enough TV to tell me, alone meant going to die. I didn't care if I died, but I wanted Luka to live, whatever it took to keep him alive.

"Don't do anything yet," he said. "I'm sending a car over now."

"No," I said vehemently. "They could be watching the house. I need to go, and it has to look like I'm going alone. Can't you just set up patrols to watch my progress?

The man thought for a moment, then said, "Keep your phone on you. I'll text you where to stop for gas, and we can correspond there."

"Good... yes, that sounds good," I replied.

"Trevor," the detective said, "please don't try to be a hero. They would've asked for money if it was a kidnapping situation. I'm guessing they want *you*, which means they have bad intentions."

"I know, but I can't put Luka in any more danger. If there's anything I can do to help..."

"Wait thirty minutes before you leave. Call me back, and I'll tell you where the first stop needs to be."

I hung up and rushed upstairs to gather some of Luka's things. I hoped I would see him and that he could use the stuff I was bringing.

I sat down in my room and wrote a letter to Aunt Doris, Peter, and Matilda, thanking them for all they'd done for me. I apologized for not waking them up, but

I knew they'd want to go, and I couldn't put Luka's life in danger in the event I was followed.

I knew this was going to feel like I'd betrayed them... but Luka had to be the priority, so I made my bed and put the letter on my pillow.

I called the detective as he'd instructed, and he told me where the first stop was along the highway. He also told me how to watch for cars that might be following me. If any were, he wanted to know ASAP.

I asked him to have an officer wake my family up after I'd left and inform them what was happening. I might be slipping out without them knowing, but at least I wanted them to know that something was going on.

When I got in my grandpa's old car, I began shaking. I was so afraid for Luka. Had I done the right thing by alerting the police? Should I have just gone on my own? It was too late now. All I could do was go and pray I'd done the right thing.

I didn't notice anyone in particular following me. I tried slowing down and speeding up, and cars either dashed around me or ignored me altogether. No vehicle seemed to be on the same road as me for long.

When I got to the first point of contact, I pulled into the gas station, filled up and rushed into the store, so anyone who was watching could see I was in a hurry.

The man behind the counter smiled at me and told me he was Officer Kent. He took my money and said, "We have patrols set up along the route. Your detective has already texted the next stop. You are to act like you have to pee. We're trying to slow you down in a way that isn't suspicious.

I nodded, took my card from him, and rushed back to my car. Putting my head in my hands for a moment, I let it all sink in. I started the car, and this time, when I pulled out, I noticed a small sedan pull out behind me.

When I pulled onto the interstate, I pressed "Call" for the detective and pushed "Speaker." "I think I'm being followed now." I described the car behind me, and the detective advised me not to try to lose him.

"Just keep an eye on him," he said. "And we'll be following close behind."

The detective advised me not to call again in case the guy following me was able to see that's what I was doing. "I'll call you if we need you, OK?" he asked.

"Yes," I answered, my voice shaking.

"Trevor, it's going to be alright. We have officers all along the route. Alabama has been alerted, and they're cooperating as well. You'll be fine. If there is any trouble, we are just moments behind you."

"OK... OK," I said again.

I hung up and turned the stereo to the station I listened to when Luka was in the car. The soft lullabies stirred up the tears that had been waiting to flow since I got the call. I let them flow, knowing this could be my last ride. Everything about this felt ominous, like I was going to meet my executioner.

The next two stops were the same. The officers were undercover and stationed in various places where I'd "accidentally" run into them while in the store. Once, I was told to put my head down like I was overcome with emotions and an officer posing as a panhandler came up to my car.

Three hours after leaving Atlanta, I pulled up to the address I'd been given. The car that had followed me the rest of the way had been pulled over by an Alabama State Trooper just before I made it to the location.

I got the detective's phone call shortly after that. "You are to drive up to the house and wait. We think the perp will call you if you just stay in the car without moving. He'll know you're afraid."

"Are there people there? Policemen?" I asked.

"Yes, the local sheriff is there along with several state troopers. We have permission to be here as well, so I'm not far behind you. We've got your back, Trevor, but you need to do this exactly like we tell you to."

"I will."

"I'm going to stay on the phone, so if he calls, put me on hold and answer. Then after he tells you what he wants you to do, you'll come back on the phone and tell me. Act like you're laying your head on the wheel when you talk to me, so he can't see you talking."

I agreed. The detective told me that when I arrived at the location, which was a red barn just like the text had stated, I was to park behind a tree where I had some cover and to wait.

As they predicted, within ten minutes of my arrival, I got a call from an unknown number, just like I had before.

When I answered, the man on the other end said, "Come in and keep your hands up so I can see them."

I made sure I hung up before speaking to the detective again. I told him what was said. "OK, wait a moment while we have the deputies come around the building. You'll be able to see them, but the perp won't. Trevor, you've got this, but if anyone tells you to drop or run, you do it, OK?"

"I understand," I said

When I saw the deputies dressed all in black come around the front of the building, I got out of the car.

I put my hands up and began walking toward the building. I'd only walked a short distance when a loud gunshot echoed through the air, followed by the screams of an infant.

It was the baby's cry that caused my brain to misfire. Instead of ducking for cover, I ran toward the building and was tackled by a large man in black... apparently one of the deputies. He held me down and told me not to move, but I was fighting against him. "I need to get to Luka! I need to get to my baby!" I cried, but the man held onto me tightly.

Within seconds there was chaos. Lights were flickering every which way, and after what seemed like ages, I heard a tinny voice coming from an earpiece the deputy holding me down had in his ear. He slowly released me but told me to stay put. Everything was under control. The baby was safe.

The second I heard that, I was struggling to get out of his arms.

"I need to see Luka," I said, and then a voice above us said, "Let him go, I've got the baby here."

The deputy let me go, and I jumped up and moved toward the voice. He handed Luka to me, and I all but swooned at having him safely in my arms. Someone was holding us up and moving us toward a chair closer to the barn.

"An ambulance is almost here. They'll check you and the baby out," he said.

No one said anything about who'd been shot or where the shot had come from, but it was only moments after the ambulances arrived that I saw them taking stretcher after stretcher out of the barn. I recognized my mother as they rushed her out. She was clearly unconscious or dead, and like with my father, I couldn't bring myself to care. Luka was in my arms... that's what mattered.

Finally, the last person to be taken out was Lisa. She was seriously hurt, and I reacted. "Lisa?" I asked, and she turned toward me. I could see the tears slip down her bruised and bloodied cheek. From where I stood, I don't think she could do much more than look at me. She was in really bad shape. I stood to go to her, but the deputy next to me placed his hand on my shoulder and said gently, "No, they need to get her to the hospital... you can see her later."

I nodded and stayed where I was. A paramedic came over and checked Luka, telling me they needed to take us both to the hospital. I nodded, and they helped me up and loaded us into the back of an ambulance.

Luka was lethargic. I'd never seen him that way, and it terrified me. They took him from me and hooked him up to IVs. "He's really dehydrated," the paramedic told me. "It appears like he hasn't eaten in a while. The IVs will help him recover."

I began shaking uncontrollably at that point, and the paramedic started working on me. They laid me down, but I resisted. I wanted to be close to Luka.

I knew enough to know I was going into shock, but I'd been without Luka for too long. I wouldn't let him be anywhere without me, ever again.

They talked me into lying down until we got to the hospital, and as long as I could see Luka, I complied.

The shaking had lessened a bit by the time we pulled up to the emergency room, and when they were unloading Luka, I got up to go with them.

"We need to treat you, Mr. Kovachich," the paramedic said.

"No, I'm not leaving Luka!" I cried.

They didn't try to stop me this time and I followed them into the ER. A paramedic was walking beside me to ensure I didn't collapse.

A team of nurses met us at the door and took over from the paramedics. Luka was rushed into a room, and I was allowed to stay with him. They put me in a chair, elevated my feet and gave me a blanket. Every so often, a nurse would check my pulse until I finally told them I was fine and to focus on the baby.

Luka's color improved, even as we sat there. My stomach was rolling, wondering how the hell this had happened. Who would take a baby and not feed him properly? Then I thought of Lisa. How was she involved... Why would she be a part of this?

The thought made my shaking return and, not wanting to be separated from Luka, I tried to calm myself, putting Lisa out of my mind.

About an hour after we arrived, the team felt comfortable enough with Luka's recovery to let me hold him. Just having him back in my arms did more to stop my shaking than anything they'd given me. I'd dozed off. I don't know how long I slept when I felt a hand on my face. I glanced up to see Peter and the tears I'd somehow managed to keep under control until then started flowing.

"We found him," I said. "We found Luka. He's going to be OK."

Peter kissed me, and Aunt Doris came around him and drew me into a hug. "Don't you ever scare me like that again," she said, loud enough to cause Luka to rouse.

When she looked down at Luka, she fell back onto the bed, and the tears flowed from her. "Oh, Trevor, you scared us so much. But Luka is OK. Thank God he's OK!"

The nurses kicked Peter and Aunt Doris out, saying they were transferring us to a room, and when we were settled, we'd all be able to be together.

Good to their word, within an hour, Luka was transferred to a room on the pediatric floor.

The hours were agony as we waited for Luka to wake up. The doctor came in and assured us it was a good sign that he reacted to noise, but he was so severely dehydrated when he came in that they were concerned about organ failure. So far, he was showing improvement.

I was too numb and out of it to even know what questions to ask. As long as Luka was in my arms, nothing else mattered.

Peter

When we arrived at the hospital, they initially refused to let me go in, saying only close family were allowed. But the detective who'd followed us in told them they needed to make an exception. Luckily, the woman behind the desk seemed to understand, and both Doris and I were able to go back to check on Trevor and see Luka.

We'd been warned we wouldn't be able to stay long. As soon as Luka was considered stable, they wanted to get him up on the floor where the pediatric doctors and nurses could work with him.

Before we were escorted up to his room, the press had begun to arrive. Luckily, there was a back entrance into the main hospital, and we were taken that way to avoid them.

Trevor wasn't well. I could tell from the moment I saw him in the ER that he wasn't the right color. I was worried about him, and when I asked the nurse, he told me they were keeping a close eye on him for possible signs of shock. I nodded and thanked him.

The entire next day, we took turns sleeping in the waiting room. Trevor refused to leave Luka's room and even refused to use the restroom unless we were there to guard the door.

He was traumatized, and I could tell he expected at any moment Luka could disappear again.

Finally, the detective arrived with a man in a sheriff's uniform. They stood at the foot of Luka's bed and told us the story.

"Lisa's father didn't know she'd been pregnant. He found out just before she gave birth, and demanded she give the baby up for adoption. He was afraid her having a baby out of wedlock would hurt his chances of remaining a deacon. Lisa didn't tell her dad you were the father, and he just assumed she'd done as he asked until your father and mother came to him asking him to help them fight to take the baby away from you." The detective cleared his throat. "They told him you were gay. Since he was afraid of losing ground with the congregation, he and your father planned to kidnap Luka and give him to a religious family here in Alabama. Everything was going to plan until you came on the news and pleaded your case. When they saw the news and you begging, it struck a nerve with your mom. When the reporter said something about your lifestyle, that somehow convinced your mother of your willingness to change. She and your father were going back on the plan and were going to take Luka home, so basically, Lisa's father shot him and beat your mom up, breaking her legs so she couldn't move."

Trevor shook his head. "I don't understand. Why...? How did they think they'd get away with it?"

"They realized they wouldn't. Lisa's parents had decided to kill everyone and commit suicide. They called you because they wanted to kill you, too."

Trevor sighed, and stared at Luka for a long moment. "What stopped them? I heard a gunshot."

The sheriff that had accompanied the detective chimed in at that point. "Luka's mother had been seriously beaten, and her dad must have thought she was dead or almost dead. He'd shot his wife earlier in the day, and apparently, he'd planted the gun he'd used to shoot her in Lisa's hand to make it look like she'd killed her own mother. Lisa spent the day in and out of consciousness, but she was able to tell us enough to know that when she realized her father planned to kill you and the baby, she came up with a plan to save you both. When he called you, it must have woken her up because she waited until he lifted his gun, then she shot him, killing him instantly."

"Lisa killed her father?" Trevor asked.

The sheriff nodded. "Apparently, she saved your life."

The tears fell from Trevor's eyes.

The lawmen glanced at each other, nodded, and took their leave. "We'll let you know more as we find out," the sheriff said.

"How's Lisa?" Trevor asked before they left.

"She's not out of the woods yet. She's had several surgeries and will need more, but they've stopped the internal bleeding."

"I want to see her," he said, shocking all of us.

"I'm afraid that's not possible, at least not yet. She's still unconscious. As soon as she recovers, they'll need to repair the fractures in her arms and legs."

The sheriff seemed to hesitate. "She's also not cleared of the kidnapping or the murder of her father. When she wakes up, she'll have to answer a lot of questions." He looked at Trevor and then down at the baby. "If we can make it happen, I'll let you know."

Then he turned and walked out of the room with the detective behind him.

Luka recovered long before Lisa did, and we were allowed to return home with him. The events had become national news, and the press was insane. Now that Luka was home, reporters were in a frenzy outside the house, lining the sidewalks while clamoring for more information. Finally, I hired a couple of off-duty police officers to stand guard to prevent the press from trying to get pictures of us through the front windows.

I was not immune. Thanks to the irresponsible news reporter we'd trusted to interview Trevor, my face was associated with the family. When I tried to go shopping for everyone, I was caught by several reporters. I ended up going home without the groceries. Joshua was a godsend during that time. He delivered what we needed to the house, and the off-duty officers brought it in for us.

Luckily, the press didn't put it together that Joshua was a friend and not just a delivery person.

A few weeks later, Lisa recovered enough to speak to the police about what had happened. The detective came by to tell us first before the press got wind of the news. "She told us how her father imprisoned her in the basement to keep her from warning us. The night they kidnapped Luka, they drugged her and kept her drugged most of the way to Alabama. Her version of events was consistent with her medical report. When everything went down, her father stopped drugging her long enough for her to, and I quote, 'see what she'd done.' He wanted to punish her for destroying his life. He beat her repeatedly until the night she texted you with the clues. She got hold of your mother's mobile phone, which she'd bought for that purpose. They didn't want to use their own phones, apparently, which is why you didn't recognize the number. Her father found the text and beat her to the point of her having internal injuries. That's when her parents figured they weren't going to get out of it. So, they planned to kill everyone, including you and the baby, and then commit suicide. Her father called you right after he beat Lisa, so she was conscious enough to hear their plan. When her father shot her mother and put the gun in Lisa's hand, she acted like she was still unconscious. Apparently, he even kicked her once or twice before he did just to make sure. I don't know how she didn't react, but she must have put on a good enough show that he thought she was dead or almost dead. You already know the rest. She woke up in time for you to arrive and somehow found the strength to shoot and kill him."

"What's going to happen to her now?" Trevor asked.

The detective shrugged. "If her story continues to hold up, she'll likely be released."

Trevor nodded. "Thank you, detective."

***

When Lisa was released, the press disappeared almost instantly, giving us freedom again to regain some of our lives.

Trevor guarded Luka like a dragon guarding treasure. The first few days after we'd arrived back at his house, he refused to put him down except to let him sleep. When Trevor began to fall asleep in his chair, his aunt took matters into her own hands and told him to lie in his bed while one of us sat with Luka. Even then, Trevor refused to let Luka outside his room. So, we took turns sitting with him.

Trevor would wake anytime we moved. His hypersensitivity couldn't be good for him, but none of us dared to suggest he take anything to calm himself. The trauma of losing Luka and the reality that he came so close to dying wasn't something anyone would be able to overcome without time.

I think it was my mother who finally made the difference. She took lunch up to Trevor one afternoon, and when she came back downstairs, she had Luka in her arms.

Doris and I stared at her. She put Luka in the bassinet that had been returned to the parlor after

Luka arrived home. Then she went about the chores she'd taken on since arriving at the house.

Neither Doris nor I had the nerve to ask what had happened for fear it would somehow disrupt the change. About an hour later, Trevor came downstairs. It was clear he'd been crying when he walked into the room. He looked at the bassinet, clearly wanting to go to Luka, but instead, he walked over and sat down next to me.

He waited, staring at the bassinet until Mom came in and sat across from him.

"I..." he started, then drew in a deep breath. "I'm afraid all the time. I close my eyes, and I see monsters stealing Luka, or worse. I realize I'm paranoid. Nothing seems to be helping so, with Matilda's advice, I've decided to have a social worker and therapist come to the house to help me." He looked around the room. "To help us overcome what happened. Matilda's right, it's not healthy for Luka to grow up in an environment of fear. He needs us... me... to get back to normal as soon as possible."

At that moment, Luka made gurgling noises in his bassinet, almost as if he were agreeing with the plan.

We all laughed, including Trevor.

We sat quietly together, all of us wanting to reach out to the baby, all of us knowing we needed to stop hovering.

Finally, Trevor interrupted the silence. "I would've died if it wasn't for you. You saved me. I'd thought of several ways to die after Luka was taken, and the longer it took for them to find him, the more I wanted to.

"You being here, it's what kept me alive and"- Trevor looked at each of us, embarrassment tinting his cheeks-"I hated you all for it." He chuckled. "I know I was a total ass, and I still have no idea why you all stayed..."

Doris went over and knelt in front of him. "We love you, Trevor." She glanced up at me and then over to my mom. "We all love you, and we love Luka."

I cleared my throat. The emotion welled up and kept me from being able to speak.

"I thought several times..." I cleared my throat, trying to regain my composure. "I thought I should go and leave you alone, especially when you were telling the truth about how I'd..." I drew in a deep breath, and Trevor leaned over against me.

"I was really angry with the world, Peter. I blamed everyone for what had happened, but I blamed myself the most. But, Peter, you aren't to blame. Neither am I or anyone else in this room." He looked at his aunt in a meaningful way. "My parents and Lisa's parents... they're the bad guys in this story, and they are never going to be a threat to Luka or us again."

Doris glanced over at Trevor, and he nodded. "Yes, my mom's still out there, but her attorneys think her psychological state is never going to be right again. She hasn't stopped ranting and raving about nonsense since that night. Besides, one of her legs had to be amputated because of infection, and the other is always going to give her trouble. Even if she gets a light sentence, she isn't going to be a threat to Luka or me ever again."

Doris lowered her head as a tear fell from her cheek.

Trevor put his hand on her shoulder. "Aunt Doris, she's your sister. You love her in a way I never have and never can. I'll never begrudge you any attention you give her, as long as we both agree it should never involve me or Luka."

She stood up and hugged him. "Agreed."

"I need to get my life back in order," he said. "That means I need to be able to function here without all of you." When he glanced around the room, he laughed. "You guys look like I just punched you all in the stomach."

"Trevor, honey," Mom chimed in, "I agree you need to get back to a normal life. I said so myself just a while ago, but are you sure you don't need help for a bit longer?"

"Mrs. Reed..." Trevor hesitated. "Matilda, if the truth be known, I'd move the two of you in full-time and hide away in fear for the rest of my life. But, if I do that, Luka will never be a normal kid. I've got to learn to trust that he isn't in danger from everyone in the world. Besides, you all have your own lives. Peter, you have to find another job, and Matilda, you have a home in Austin. Aunt Doris and I also have to get back to living our lives. And she has to reconnect with Leonardo."

Doris appeared shocked and more tears fell from her eyes. "He might've been told to go away and never come back," Doris said as she buried her head in her hands.

Mom went over and sat next to her. "Oh, honey, he'll understand, the pressure here was intense."

"I agree," I told her. "He's texted me almost every day since Luka was kidnapped. Did you know he stopped all work on the project until now?"

Trevor looked at me. "He did what?"

"Yeah, he was so overcome with concern, he stopped the project dead in its tracks until Luka was found."

"Has he started back up yet?"

I shook my head. "I don't think so. I think he'd have told me if he had."

Trevor sighed. "Can you invite him over for dinner tomorrow, Peter? He needs some closure around this as well."

I nodded. "I'll text him now and see."

The next day, Richmond showed up with wine. He'd clearly lost some weight since the last time we'd seen him. He walked in, and when he saw Luka lying in the bassinet, he caught his breath and turned. "I don't deserve to be here," he said.

Doris caught him and pulled him into a hug. "It isn't your fault. I'm sorry I blamed you," she said.

Trevor picked Luka up and walked over to Richmond. "Sit down, Leonardo," he commanded, and the big man did as he was told.

Trevor put Luka in his arms. "It's about time you held your nephew," he said, then looked meaningfully at his aunt.

The older man blushed and appeared to be the most uncomfortable person on the planet as he held Luka. The baby was as content as could be and snuggled comfortably into the big man's arms. As he stared down at the infant, the fear on his face was quickly replaced with the same joy any loving adult had when seeing a little one.

When Richmond looked back up, he asked, "How can you want me to be his uncle when I'm the reason you were all distracted?"

Trevor smiled. "If it hadn't been then, it'd have been another time. Besides, Luka needs family, and anyone who loves him enough to put his life on hold while we searched for him loves him enough to be family."

The man sucked in a breath, clearly trying not to let his emotions get the best of him.

"Now, you and Aunt Doris have baby duty while the rest of us get dinner finished."

He glanced at Trevor, then over at Doris, who was blushing like a virgin on her wedding day.

When we came back in, Doris and Richmond were sitting on the antique sofa. Doris held Luka, and Richmond had his arm around her. Both were staring at the baby like they were the only three people in the world.

Mom tapped Trevor's shoulder and whispered, "You are a smart one. You know that man will be gaga over that little one for the rest of his life, don't you?"

"I'm hoping that's true. Family is important, and Luka deserves people who love him."

Mom smiled at him, then over at me, giving me a meaningful look. "That's my belief as well."

After we'd eaten, Trevor turned to Richmond. "I want you to start the project again. I also want the damned reporters to stop asking questions every time any of us go outside the house."

"At least they aren't camped outside on the front lawn any longer," Doris chimed in.

We all nodded. "Well, they aren't going away until we give them what they want. So, here's my idea. Leonardo, let's get your project going again. We can hold a press conference and be there with Luka to show the world we are all OK, and everything is back the way it's supposed to be."

Richmond turned toward me and shrugged. "I'm afraid I've got some bad news on that front." He looked over at the rest of the folks in the room. "I fired my architectural firm. The person I wanted to run my project was fired from the firm just a few weeks after starting. Until I hire another architect, I'm afraid the project is on hold." He brought his gaze back to me in what appeared to be a question.

"I can help you find someone, but I'm afraid even though I was fired, they still have a two-year, two-hundred-mile non-compete that appears to be ironclad."

Richmond nodded. "Yes, I've had my attorneys looking into that as well, but in my contract, I specifically said you were the lead architect on the project, and I wouldn't work with anyone else. Since they fired you, it was in direct breach of our contract. My attorneys have already sent them notice that I intend to file a breach of contract lawsuit with them."

I shook my head. "I'm not sure what that means."

He laughed a little too loudly and quickly caught himself, glancing over at the sleeping baby before continuing. "It means if they don't want to be sued for a three-million-dollar breach of contract lawsuit that's cost me several million more in delays on projects outside of this one, then they'll have to negotiate."

"Do you think they'll do that?" I asked. "Do you really want to work with me after all that chaos?"

"Frankly, you are the *only* architect I want to work with. The other people I talked to at your old firm were totally incompetent and had no idea what I wanted. I hired your firm because of your past projects and because you understand the mix of old and new that's needed for my stores to be successful. So, what do you say, are you willing to come to work for me again?"

I smiled. "I... I don't know what to say."

Mom leaned over and playfully tapped the back of my head. "The answer is yes, dear."

"Yes, dear," I said to Richmond, and we all laughed before checking our noise level.

"Now, if I can talk a certain couture shop owner into merging her store with mine, I'll have exactly what I need to make this thing a success."

Trevor looked over at his aunt. "He wants to combine couture with steampunk?"

Doris blushed. "Well, it really is a good fit, even Dad would've been proud to work with him. It's kitschy and modern..."

Doris seemed to notice she'd pretty much begun trying to sell me on the idea when she stopped herself. "What do you think, Trevor? The shop was meant to go to you if I didn't want it... Dad didn't want me to push you into it, and you've never shown interest."

"Would you like it more if it was aligned with Leonardo's shop?"

She shook her head. "I don't like the stuff coming out of Italy. It doesn't seem to match the flow of the city today. Dad's customers are slowly growing too old, or they're dying, so if we don't do something it'll probably fail in a few years anyway. Besides, the movie industry in Atlanta is really steaming up. This type of design would be right down their alley."

Trevor got up and hugged his aunt. "You have my blessing. Besides, after it goes through, can I start calling Leonardo, Uncle Leo?'"

Doris stared at him as if he'd slapped her. Her mouth was agape. Richmond blushed as well, and when neither responded, Trevor said, "You know, they say a business merger is like a marriage, so it stands to reason if you two *merge*, he'd be an uncle to me as well as Luka!"

Doris stood up and went into the kitchen, calling out behind her, "I'm getting more wine, and Trevor, you have trash duty for the next month... no, *make that the next year*!"

When she disappeared, the group laughed out loud again. No one needed to worry since Luka was awake and playing with his feet.

Mom reached over and picked him up. "Hello, beautiful, were you enjoying the show?" she asked, and Luka babbled in her arms.

Trevor

"Peter, can you come with me up to the attic?" I asked. I hadn't been up there since Luka was taken and I wanted to talk to Peter alone.

He turned toward me, concern clearly visible on his face, but nodded before standing. I wanted to ask Matilda to watch Luka, but I also wanted to show that I could just trust that he'd be OK. I knew it was going to be a long time before I didn't have to force myself to trust, but at least I could be away from him without having a panic attack.

When we got to the door leading into the attic, I reached over and grabbed Peter's hand. As I drew in a deep breath, Peter asked if this was my first time up there since it happened.

I nodded. "OK, let's get this over with," I said and pushed the door open.

Nothing had changed since that night. The nanny's knitting was still on the floor where she'd dropped it. The sight of that alone would have been enough to force me back down the stairs, never to return. Instead, I drew in another deep breath and forced myself to continue forward.

The rest of the room was less ominous. And as I'd hoped, it reminded me more of the comfortable place it had been rather than the place where Luka had been taken.

I walked over to the makeshift sitting room and asked Peter to sit across from me.

"Peter," I began, "how long has it been since you slept in your own condo?"

Peter glanced over at me in surprise. "Um..." he said. "I'm not sure, maybe a few weeks. Why? Are you ready for me... us to get out of your hair?"

I looked at him for a long moment. "No, I'm asking you to move in."

Peter gulped. "Um... Trevor, I don't know. That's a huge commitment for two men who just started... um... you know."

I chuckled. "I'm not asking you to move in as my lover. I'm asking you to move in as someone who loves Luka."

"But," he said, still obviously struggling with the concept, "we... we are lovers, or at least we used to be."

"I'm aware of that," I admitted. "But, I'm also aware of the fact that during this whole mess, you've been steadfast even when I was telling you to go. I can't take care of Luka by myself. At least not the way I want to. If I'd been more diligent, then it's unlikely the person caring for him would've let someone like my father into this room. Even though she was drugged, the nanny could've called for help that night. She didn't know us well enough to know my father was dangerous. It was only natural that she'd let a baby's grandfather in. I've been thinking a lot about it. I've talked to Aunt Doris about it, too. The house is mostly paid for. We don't have to pay much to keep the lights on and water running, and it would never hurt to have an architect on site to keep the old lady up to par. If you'd be willing to help with Luka, we'd only charge you your share of the utilities."

"Bullshit," he said. "If I move in, I'll pay rent like any decent human being. I'll help with Luka 'cause I care about him. Not because I want to save money."

I'll admit, seeing Peter become indignant made me feel better. I was hoping he cared about Luka like he was family, but I wasn't sure.

"Then, tell me what you think about this space," I said.

Peter looked around. "You already know I think this is one of the best spaces in the house. The huge ceilings, open concept, geez," he said while spinning around in the chair. "It's almost the size of the entire second floor."

"Then, I'd like to offer this space to you as your own private apartment."

Peter thought for a few moments. "The truth is, that could be a big problem. I'm in love with you, Trevor. I'd love to live in the same home as you, but I want you in my arms. While you've been going through hell, I've mourned for you, watched you suffer, and I haven't been able to take it away, but through it all, I just wanted to hold you, comfort you... It wasn't appropriate, and I couldn't do it when you were so angry, but I wanted it, nonetheless. If I move in, I won't be moving in as a roommate, I'll be moving in as your mate. I know that might not be what you want to hear, but for me, it's all or nothing."

After all the tears I'd shed this past month, none had come because I was feeling loved or wanted... most came as the inner voice of criticism seeped into my brain, telling me how worthless I was as a parent... but these tears flowed because this incredible man was sitting across from me, telling me he wouldn't compromise.

I lowered my face. "Peter, it's too early. I know it is, but I don't want you to go back to your condo. I'm willing for you to move in as my lover... my companion, if you are."

Peter stood up and pulled me into his arms. "Yes, I'll do it. I don't want to live without you either."

Epilogue – Two Years Later: Trevor

The wedding was going to be incredible. The entire store was covered in steampunk-themed décor. Aunt Doris was beautiful in her gown that was, incidentally, designed by her soon-to-be husband. I'm not sure what the good luck rule was on the husband designing the dress, but if the last two years were any indication, their relationship was only likely to get better with time.

Luka drooled on my tux. He had every ounce of the terrible twos, but unfortunately for everyone involved, it hit at around eighteen months. He was everywhere and could move faster than any little person should be able to move. It usually required every set of available eyes to keep him from disappearing.

Leonardo came up to us, and Luka spotted him and screamed, "Uncle Weo!" Without a moment of hesitation, Leonardo grabbed him up, kissing him and causing him to squeal. Since he'd been declared an honorary uncle, the two had been almost inseparable.

I'd started calling him Uncle Leo after that night, and it was the source of a lot of embarrassment for my aunt, which caused me to behave worse than ever.

Peter had gone to work for Leonardo after that night as well. Peter's old firm quickly settled by making an exception for the project. Peter had been the lead architect on all the shops that now spanned both the East and West coasts of the US and Canada.

When Luka was a little over a year old, he'd started calling Leonardo, Uncle Weo, and the name had stuck. Peter tended to call him Uncle Weo now, too, just to tease his new employer. A couple of magazine spreads had even caught word of it and asked if Leonardo and Luka could pose for the article they were doing on Leonardo's new family.

It was a big shock to the world that the infamous bachelor had decided to settle down, but Aunt Doris had come into the public limelight like the regal queen she was.

The two were in love. In fact, if I weren't so in love myself, I'd say it was a disgusting amount of love. But whenever Peter was around, I couldn't keep my hands off him. I was still surprised someone like me could catch a beautiful man like him.

And the press had homed in on him as well. There were several spreads about Leonardo's designs that featured the increasingly popular and mysterious architect Peter Reed.

Joshua had become a member of the family, too, and shortly after all the crap went down with Lisa's parents and mine, we declared him Luka's official godparent. There was even a big ceremony to celebrate. Luka loved Joshua, and the two would get together at least once a week to play with the homemade blocks Joshua brought him.

I continued my work as a PI. After nearly losing Luka, I knew firsthand how important it was for people to have a resource to keep track of anyone who was acting weird or strange. I focused my career on helping those in trouble, and those who couldn't protect themselves, and as a result, I'd become pretty familiar with the Atlanta Police Department.

The detective on Luka's case checked in frequently about cases he either couldn't pursue or didn't have the resources that my company did. My boss was exceptionally sympathetic to my work and let me get away with working pro bono from time to time. When confronted, she'd shrug and say, "You brought us into a working relationship with the Atlanta Police Department. That's worth more than the few bucks a client would bring in. Just remember, we still have to pay for the lights, though." Then she'd chuckle since we both knew the woman wasn't short of money.

Leonardo had Peter redesign the shop to include upstairs offices, saying he could use the revenue to offset the costs of the building. However, I know he did it to give Peter his own space to work from.

When Aunt Doris moved in with Leonardo, a year before they got married, it opened the house up to our growing family. Matilda hadn't sold her home in Austin, but she spent a good portion of the year with us. The house was so big, though, we didn't get in each other's way much.

Peter had turned the attic into a luxury master bedroom. It maximized the large living space, giving us a small kitchenette, a detached nursery, and a massive en suite bathroom and master closet. He also built in an elevator that utilized the old butler's closet and delivered Matilda to her bedroom on the second floor. With Luka becoming a squirming monster, trying to haul him up and down the stairs had quickly become precarious, to say the least, so the elevator helped to keep him at bay and allowed us to secure the stairs in a way that prevented him from accidentally going down them.

You wouldn't think a two-year-old could get in and out of a room, but trust me, the boy was a master escape artist. He could open any door that hadn't been designed specifically to keep him out.

When Lisa was discharged from the hospital, Peter and I were there to pick her up. After losing her parents, she really didn't have anyone left. Her parents had alienated everyone in her life, including her grandparents. And since she'd been the one to shoot her father, even though it was to save us, she would likely never have a relationship with them.

I was determined to recruit her to be a part of Luka's life, but the truth was, I missed her, too. We'd been best friends since elementary school. Just like how my family, Peter and Matilda had stood up for me when I needed them, I was going to be that for Lisa.

She was not an easy code to crack, though. The trauma of what happened weighed heavily. After she sold her parents' estate and inherited their savings, she put herself in a program that helped people overcome post-traumatic stress disorder.

She stayed with us off and on, but just as we began to get close, she'd end up running away, and every time she'd have to spend time in the program again.

About a month ago, Lisa introduced me to one of her therapists, who requested Lisa have a family counseling session with me. During the session, I gathered some insight into why she was struggling so much with reconnecting. She continued to blame herself for what happened, and when she gave herself permission to reconnect, she'd spiral down into a depression and have to start over again.

During the session, I was able to tell her how much I loved her and how much I'd always wanted her to be a part of Luka's life.

It was then that she shared a part of the story that always seemed to confuse me.

After she gave Luka to me, she went back to live with her parents because she didn't have anywhere else to go. She'd dropped out of college so she couldn't get a job that paid enough for her to live independently.

Her parents punished her for having a baby out of wedlock by telling her if she ever went out without them chaperoning, they'd kick her out onto the streets.

I asked her why she didn't just come live with us, and she came clean, saying part of her knew her father would become violent if he ever found out it was me that was Luka's dad. He'd resented me throughout her childhood because I was a friend outside the church. She knew if he found out I was bisexual, he'd become... well, what he became.

Staying away was the only way she knew how to keep Luka and me safe. It saddened me that she'd known he was what he was and that she stayed with her family instead of turning to us. I didn't say anything, though, knowing it could make the situation worse. But if she'd trusted me, I know we could've kept both sets of our parents away.

The therapist sat with me a moment after Lisa left to join a group session and told me that if it wasn't for me and Luka, Lisa wouldn't be progressing as well as she was. "Sometimes, the best catalyst to change is conflict. You and Luka are what drives her to keep working at it. I know it may not seem like it, but your commitment toward her gives her that hope."

With those words, I continued to keep the pressure on Lisa to be a part of our lives, letting her know she was always welcome. It was just a few weeks after the session, and right before the wedding, that Luka called her mama for the first time. It was then I saw a light turn on that I hadn't seen since before we'd had Luka. My prayer was that that light was the one that would lead to Lisa's healing.

Peter proposed to me the day after New Year's, the anniversary of when Luka became my sole responsibility. We'd gone to the little diner that had become a regular haunt of ours. I noticed everyone seemed to be acting strange, a couple of the servers even chuckled and blushed when they looked my way.

Catherine, the owner, and the woman who served me on that fateful day, walked us over to the very table I'd sat at with Lisa. I gave Peter a look.

"What are you up to, Peter Reed?" I asked, knowing something was happening.

This was one of the busiest days for Catherine. It was always a busy place, but the day after a holiday, people tended to just want comfort food without a lot of splash, so the fact the place was empty tipped me off further.

Peter fell to one knee, pulled a ring box out of his pocket, and opened it. "Trevor Kovachich, I've never loved anyone as much as I love you... well, except maybe Luka, but besides him, you make me happy in every way possible. I wake up every day and thank whatever gods are listening that I get to hold you in my arms when I wake up and cuddle you when we sleep. I can't imagine any other man I'd want in my life more than I want you. So, would you please marry me and be my husband forever?" he asked.

I stared at him, dumbfounded. It's not like I didn't know we might get married someday. Hell, we'd discussed it several times since he'd moved in, but it never seemed like the right time. Luka took too much of our time, and then there was Peter's work.

It must have appeared as if I hesitated, and I watched as Peter's face fell. I couldn't help it, I laughed out loud. "Like I'd ever say no to you." I fell to my knees in front of him, took the ring box, and wrapped my arms around him, kissing him with everything I had in me.

When I pulled back, Peter had a dreamy expression on his face. "We're really gonna get married?" he asked.

"Seems like it," I said, and kissed him again.

We heard someone clear their throat behind us and looked up to see our entire family, including Lisa, standing in the restaurant.

A huge cheer went up when I made a spectacle of slipping the ring on my finger.

There was a huge party, and more of our friends and coworkers showed up to celebrate with us. When the place was filled to the brim, I asked, "What would you have done if I said no?"

"I'd have kicked your ass, then thrown you over my shoulder like a caveman. I already had plans to haul you down to the courthouse for a shotgun wedding."

Matilda leaned over. "I have the shotgun in my car." And then she smirked.

For some reason, I thought the joke might not have been much of a joke. Peter might not have it in him to force me to marry him. Matilda, on the other hand, was capable of anything.

Peter asked me if I'd consider getting married on the anniversary of finding Luka. "That's the day when everything went from darkness to light," he said. "I'd like to commemorate it with the next-best day of my life."

I readily agreed. I knew we all remembered the time Luka had been gone, and we tended to avoid each other during those days. I loved the idea of turning that ominous anniversary into one of celebration.

When I mentioned it to Lisa, wanting to make sure it was something she could handle, she burst into tears. "That's the best thing you could do!" she agreed. "I hate that day, more than any other of the year. If I could celebrate it with my best friend who lived despite my father's hatred, it would make me happier than anything else in the world."

I teased her. "Better than a chocolate shake with strawberries and whipped cream?"

"I can't believe you remember that!" She laughed through her tears. "What were we? Twelve?

"Something like that. I still can't believe you ate all of mine when I went to the restroom."

"Serves you right for telling Ashton Christianson I had a crush on him."

"You did have a crush on him. In fact, you wouldn't shut up about it."

"Yeah, but you aren't supposed to tell. God, Trevor, it's a miracle you didn't scar me for life."

"Psss, you're the toughest broad I've ever known," I said with humor.

"Well, used to know. No one is tougher than Matilda."

We both laughed out loud and hugged.

"Thank you, Trevor."

"You're welcome, Mama..."

"Oh no, you are not Mike Pence! I am not going to be called 'mama' by my baby daddy."

I choked. "Baby daddy? What the fuck?"

Lisa roared with laughter. "Well, that's what you are!"

"Don't ever call me that again!"

"Then you agree never to call me mama again."

"Deal, I'll just call you, bitch!"

She poked me in the ribs. "I can still kick your ass, Trevor Kovachich. Hey, are you going to take Peter's name?"

"No, believe it or not, he's taking mine. Peter Reed Kovachich."

"Why would anyone in their right mind become a Kovachich?" she teased.

"Because he's in love with me... and you should be so lucky!" I teased.

"That's true," she said, and hugged me. "It sucks that we got drunk that night and did what we did, but I wouldn't change it now. Luka is the best thing that's ever happened to us."

I hugged her back. "Truer words were never spoken."

I had been lost in thought as I looked over at Lisa, who was now sitting across from me at Aunt Doris and Leo's wedding and winked at her. She smiled back, then looked back up as my aunt said "I do" while gazing in her new husband's eyes.

That day, as I watched my aunt and now-official uncle celebrate their relationship with their family, friends, and the world, I couldn't help but want that for me and Peter and Luka, too.

I looked down at the engagement ring on my finger and smiled. Peter Reed was mine, I was his and Luka... he was ours.

***

Continue Reading for an excerpt from
Taking A Chance For Love

TAKING A CHANCE FOR LOVE

Blake Allwood

Prologue – Twenty Years Earlier

The trees were so heavy with fruit, the limbs barely swayed as the hot arid breeze drifted through their branches.

I screamed happily as my uncle found me hidden underneath one of the trees. "You're it!" he exclaimed, and ran as I chased him.

"I'm faster than you, Uncle Chris," I yelled, but my great-uncle was already hidden, even though he always hid in the same spot, making it easy for me to find him.

The crew working nearby glanced at one another, then chuckled as I ran by them. I lingered just long enough to hear them talking.

"Chris is crazy about that boy," I heard one of them say.

The response, however, was what any young boy who adored his uncle would want to hear. The comment left me feeling like I truly had a place in this life.

"Bet he ends up growing up just like him."

The first thick drops of the monsoon storm began falling, and Uncle Chris grabbed me from behind, causing me to squeal.

As we ran toward the house, he said, just barely out of breath, "Your mama's gonna skin us both if I get you back soaked to the bone again."

"Not me," I giggled, as I bounced in my uncle's arms. "But she'll skin you." And we both laughed when she opened the door, shaking her head.

"I swear you're just as bad as him," she said to Uncle Chris, as she moved back, allowing us both in, dripping on the tiles of her entryway.

"I've already left the towels there on the back of the chair. Make sure you take your shoes off before you come in," she said, no heat in her command. It wasn't needed, since both of us had gotten a good lecture the day before, when we'd come in tracking sandy sludge across her living room.

"When you two are done drying off, come on in. I've just finished making scones. You can both have one, and hopefully, it won't spoil your dinner."

Dad slipped in the back door when mom wasn't looking, and pulled her into a wet embrace causing her to scream, which ended in laughter. "I swear, the lot of you are gonna be the end of me," she exclaimed, before darting out of his arms, and returned to the marmalade I could smell cooking on the stove.

As we sat around the kitchen table, I was overcome with happiness and I looked between Dad and Uncle Chris, and said, "I'm the luckiest boy in Mesa," causing both men to smile.

Mom came over and rubbed my head, and replied, "I'd say we're all pretty lucky." She turned loving eyes toward Dad, whose smile reflected the same emotion back at her.

That's what I'd loved, and that's what I'd lost. Our life under the trees had been a place of happiness and peace, the kind that my entire family seemed to feel deep in our hearts.

Chapter One
Joshua – Present Day

"Are you Joshua Howard?" the man asked, as I stood staring at the casket at the bottom of the open grave. Most of the other funeral attendees had already left, but I'd stayed back, the shock of my Uncle Chris's death still swirling through me.

"Yeah," I responded, but didn't look his way.

"I'm Cecil Arlington with Arlington, Hush, and Langley," he informed me.

I turned to him then, wondering why someone would tell me his professional name, while standing next to a grave.

"Your uncle put you in his will. Can you come by my office before you leave?" he asked briskly, then handed me his card. "You can call this number and set up a time with my assistant."

I stared at the card as he left. What on earth did my uncle leave me? I guessed the better question was, why would my uncle leave me anything? It isn't like we were close—at least not any longer. I'd moved to Atlanta with my parents when I was a pre-teen and hadn't seen him again.

I'd wondered all these years why I'd never heard from him. Was he so angry with my father that he didn't want me in his life either?

I'd begun trying to find him once I'd gotten old enough to do things without my father looking over my shoulder, but I'd never had much luck. Finally, I hired my friend, Trevor, who worked as a private investigator, to see what he could find. Within a week he'd located him, and with the information he'd given me, I'd reached out. That was just a few weeks ago.

My uncle had seemed genuinely happy to speak with me. He never told me he was sick. Instead, all he seemed to want to talk about was when I was younger, running amuck around the orange groves where he worked. He promised to get back in touch with me, but he never did.

I tried calling his home several times, but never got through again. I figured he'd had his talk and was done with me, then a few days ago, I got a call from a woman named Melinda, who said she was dealing with his messages. She was the one that told me he'd passed away, and gave me the details of the funeral.

Depression overtook me. My uncle was the last of my family. My father didn't count. Not really. Even my friends called him a statue. I spent the next couple days managing my anxiety. I knew it was ridiculous to mourn someone I didn't really know, but for me this was the loss of hope that I'd ever have a family. If I was being honest, it really represented the loss of a belief I'd secretly held onto, that once I was reconnected with my uncle, I'd reclaim all the happiness I'd once had as a child.

After I'd navigated all my emotions and the initial shock, I called my father to ask if he wanted to go with me. With his ever-present stoic, businesslike politeness, he declined.

I took a deep breath, knowing I was gonna get lashed by his temper, but asked anyway, "Dad, what was the problem between you two?"

"Nothing that concerns you," he snapped, making it clear the conversation was over.

If my uncle was anything like my dad, they'd probably had a fight over who was more stubborn or willful. Apparently, my dad won, since here I was standing by my uncle's open grave...alone.

I looked at the card again and sat down on one of the plastic chairs the funeral home had put out for people to sit on. As I appeared to be alone now, I decided to have a final talk with my uncle, even though I knew he couldn't answer.

"Uncle Chris, what happened? Why didn't you tell me you were sick? Why didn't you—?"

I stopped abruptly when I noticed a man was walking toward me and the grave. When he was only a few feet away, he stopped and stood watching me. Had I not known better, I'd have said he was checking me out, although, I couldn't imagine a tear-streaked man sitting by an open grave and talking to a dead man in a casket was a very attractive sight.

I put my head in my hands and continued speaking, this time quieter since I didn't appreciate the audience. "Uncle, I spent so many years looking for you. I missed you all that time, but I didn't know how to reach you..."

I sat there until the funeral home's men came to fill the grave in. Not having the stomach to watch them, I walked back to my car. The guy who'd been there was now gone, which was good. I wanted to be on my own, and even if he'd known my uncle, I didn't want to hear about a man who hadn't been a part of my life, or worse, hear about how my uncle had been a mentor or father figure in someone else's life, a life that by all rights should've been mine.

I climbed into my rental and drove to a business parking lot nearby, where I let more tears fall. The tears soon turned to anger.

After losing my mom, I'd held onto the thought that even though my dad was an unfeeling jerk, I still had an uncle who loved me. Now he was gone too!

"*I HATE THIS!*" I yelled, slamming my hands on the steering wheel.

I laid my head back, and thought of my mom who would have known just what to say. I missed her. Life wasn't fair. All that was left was *him*... a dad who never showed emotion, excluding the occasional angry outburst when things didn't go his way.

Once I got my feelings under control, I drove to my hotel, and extended my stay. I then called my dad, leaving a message when he didn't answer... not that I expected him to.

"Hey, just got back to the hotel from the funeral. Call me if you want to know how it went. Oh, also, I was approached by an attorney about Uncle Chris's estate, so I'll need to stick around a little longer. I'll call you later. Bye."

I hoped saying what I did would at least spark some kind of emotion, even a greedy reaction would be better than nothing.

I lay in bed that afternoon, thinking about my childhood, and how happy it had been. My uncle was in charge of a huge orange grove somewhere in the Mesa area. I couldn't even find the property on a map now if I wanted to, but I remembered running down the rows of trees, and around Christmas, eating my fill of freshly picked fruit.

My mom had been big on canning things, and we'd had marmalade coming out of our ears. Those were the years my father would laugh. I couldn't quite remember what that sounded like, but I do remember how happy I'd been.

My uncle used to come get me to help with chores, even during the intense heat of the summer, but we'd always stop mid-morning and eat a homemade orange popsicle. He told me you needed to love the product if you were going to be any good at producing it, so we had orange-flavored everything when we were living next to him.

I was probably nine or ten when my father and uncle fell out, but even at that age, I'd understood my life was changing. My stomach rolled with memory and resentment. There was not a lot a kid could do to stop the wheels put in motion by their adults, even if those adults were being idiots.

We'd moved to Atlanta that summer, and I thought I'd die from the humidity. Mesa was hot as Hades, but nothing like Atlanta's heat. I kept asking Mom if I could go back to help Uncle Chris in the fall, and she always shook her head and looked sad, the way she did whenever I mentioned him.

After a while, I stopped asking, then she got sick, and within a few months, she was gone as well.

That was when Dad stopped being Dad. He disappeared into himself, and although he provided for me, kids needed love as well as groceries. That didn't seem to matter though, my dad had turned into an emotional shell. I was eleven when Mom died. I was so angry that I'd lost so much in such a short time. I'd rail at my dad, I'd throw tantrums... but no matter what I did, he never even seemed to notice, or care. Eventually, I learned to live without connections to other humans. My happy place became the memories of my past—the place I escaped to in my mind.

With Uncle Chris's death, all the hope I'd held onto for all those years was dead now too, and I felt lost, empty, and downright pissed off about it.

***

Purchase **Taking A Chance For Love** now at:
blakeallwood.com/booklink/2077809

Looking for more books by #ownvoice authors?

Check out
lgbtqownvoice.com

Made in the USA
Coppell, TX
13 July 2022